"Would you let me shoot you?"

"I bet you'd like to," Devlin said dryly, interpreting Cressy literally. "I thought you concentrated on wildlife."

"You are wildlife. A panther, remember? You'd make an interesting study of domestic adaptation."

His eyes narrowed, the predator sizing up the prey. "I might consider it—providing you agree not to try and run off again. Stay a few more days until Chester can discharge his medical responsibilities with a clear conscience. The police might even get your gear back before you leave."

Cressy knew she wasn't in any condition to work yet...today had proved it. But to stay here—that would be courting the danger she'd been so anxious to escape. And she wasn't thinking about physical danger!

Susan Napier was born on Valentine's Day, so perhaps it is only fitting that she become a romance writer. She started out as a reporter for New Zealand's largest evening newspaper before resigning to marry the paper's chief reporter. After the birth of their two children, she did some free-lancing for a film-production company and then settled down to write her first romance. "Now," she says, "I am in the enviable position of being able to build my career around my home and family."

Books by Susan Napier

HARLEQUIN PRESENTS
1211—ANOTHER TIME
1252—THE LOVE CONSPIRACY
1284—A BEWITCHING COMPULSION
1332—FORTUNE'S MISTRESS
1380—NO REPRIEVE
1460—DEAL OF A LIFETIME

HARLEQUIN ROMANCE
2711—LOVE IN THE VALLEY
2723—SWEET VIXEN

Don't miss any of our special offers. Write to us at the following address for information on our newest releases.

Harlequin Reader Service
P.O. Box 1397, Buffalo, NY 14240
Canadian address: P.O. Box 603,
Fort Erie, Ont. L2A 5X3

SUSAN NAPIER

devil to pay

Harlequin Books

TORONTO • NEW YORK • LONDON
AMSTERDAM • PARIS • SYDNEY • HAMBURG
STOCKHOLM • ATHENS • TOKYO • MILAN
MADRID • WARSAW • BUDAPEST • AUCKLAND

For Elizabeth and George Grove.

Harlequin Presents first edition August 1992
ISBN 0-373-11483-4

Original hardcover edition published in 1991
by Mills & Boon Limited

DEVIL TO PAY

CHAPTER ONE

By THE time Cressida had stripped down to her slip she knew she was in trouble.

She blinked at the wavering ribbon of country road unwinding ahead of her, her fingers slipping damply on the steering-wheel of her rented car. It was hot...so hot. Even with the air-conditioning on cold and the driver's window wide open she was still sweltering. Sweat glistened on her bare shoulders and slid down between her breasts, making the slip stick uncomfortably to her skin. She cast a longing look at the empty six-pack of soft drinks on the passenger seat beside her, lying on her progressively discarded skirt and blouse. She had needed the drinks, not only to quench her raging thirst, but to hold against the fiery skin of her throat and face in a vain attempt to transfer some of their blessed icy coolness to her body.

She was beyond berating herself for starting out on this trip when she'd known she wasn't well. In fact, at this point she was pretty much beyond *anything*. The only thing that kept her going was the knowledge that she had a job to do. She had a deadline. She had made a promise and Cressida Cross always, *always* kept her promises. Being ill was boring. It put you at the mercy of others. And, more importantly, it wasted time that you usually couldn't afford.

A logging truck passed her going the other way, the thundering roar giving way to a sucking force that buffeted the little car, making the roiling in her stomach worse. Concentrating on controlling it, Cressy didn't even notice that she had taken a wrong fork. It was so *hot*...! She had thought of taking off her slip, too, but some hazy vestige of common sense stopped her. Her purple slip might just scrape through as a dress at a brief glance from a passing car, but her bra and panties were far too lacy to be decent. Cressy didn't know what the local customs were, but flaunting of a female body could gain you a nasty sentence in some parts of the world.

No, that wasn't right. Cressy frowned. Of course she knew what the customs were. She was back in New Zealand. Home. She blinked a drop of sweat out of her eye. It was the heat that had confused her. This was more like equatorial jungle stuff than springtime Down Under.

The road was very narrow and windy. She frowned again. The Hauraki Plains were flat. The roads were supposed to be long and wide and straight, great for speeding. How long since she had left Auckland? The whole trip was only supposed to take four hours. It felt as if she had been on the road for ten. Where was her map?

With her left hand she rummaged among the cans and hurriedly changed her mind as the car pulled, jolting her arm painfully, almost wrenching the wheel from her sweaty grip. It took an effort with both hands to straighten up. Was she just tired, or did the little car suddenly seem very heavy? Maybe she should stop and check the tyres, especially since an ominous bank of cloud was boiling up over the horizon. Check your equipment. Always check your equipment...

Cressy pulled over, towards the thorny hedge which grew almost to the edge of the narrow road. Too late she noticed the grassy dip that indicated a ditch. The car jolted to a stop, slamming her forwards against her seatbelt.

The car was on a tilt and it took a struggle for Cressy to push her door open and stumble out. Only the left front wheel was in the ditch, but she knew she wouldn't be able to get it out without help. The road was empty and everything seemed very quiet.

The first drops of rain were deliciously cool against her skin. Within minutes the temperature dropped dramatically, but Cressy, wrapped in her envelope of fever, didn't feel it. She would have to walk for help, she decided. It would be good to stretch her legs after being cramped behind the wheel for so long.

She opened the back door of the car and picked up a small, battered black case that fitted into her hand like an extra appendage. Her precious OM-1. The first real camera she had ever possessed. Her charm. Her baby. All the other gear, the heavy bag of practical rather than sentimental stuff, she covered up with the car rug. She didn't have the energy to carry anything else, except spare film, of course. Even in a stupor she didn't forget one of the first rules of photography. She stuffed the little plastic cylinder down between her breasts and was careful to make sure all the doors were locked.

It was only when she had shut the door again that she realised that she was still only wearing her slip. She giggled. Stupid thing to do. She laughed even harder when she realised that she had locked the keys in the car and she couldn't get to her clothes. Some farmer was going to get an eyeful! Well, if she couldn't get into her car nor could anyone else. At least she was wearing shoes—the black ballet slippers she used for driving. She didn't have her bag but she had the most important thing, her favourite camera.

The rain came down harder, colder, as she trudged along the stony verge, but to Cressy it felt like a warm shower. She could practically feel it hissing as it touched her flaming skin.

It was late afternoon but the darkened sky made it seem nearer to dusk. The gravel at the edge of the road ripped at her soft shoes but Cressy didn't notice. The camera in its case rapped against her as she walked, tangling in the long, thick plait that hung down her back, but she didn't notice that, either. She was concentrating on putting one foot in front of the other and discovered to her delight that she wasn't walking, she was floating...

She almost floated right past the steel gates on the other side of the road without even seeing them. A high dry-stone wall ran as far as she could see in either direction into the gathering mist. Through the gates she could see the shadowy outline of a big house. And lights. Lights meant kindness and shelter...

Hitching her camera strap on her shoulder, Cressy carefully looked both ways before she crossed the road.

The gates were locked with a chain. Cressy was angry. What did they do that for? She reached out to rattle the gates and found herself sitting suddenly on the ground, her wet hands hurting, her whole body tingling unpleasantly, her head buzzing as if it would burst. At first she thought she'd been struck by lightning, but then she realised: the gates were electrified!

Cressy went from bewilderment to outrage. She had come here for help and the people in that house had tried to kill her?

Cressy got up with difficulty. Her throat was too thick and sore to say the words she wanted to, so she looked around for another method of expression. There was a glint in the grass verge a few metres up the road. She marched unsteadily up and investigated it. Part of a car bumper, bent and corroded. It made her feel dizzy but none the less she doggedly dragged it to the gates, lifted it up, staggering under the weight, and threw it with all the power of her fury at the mocking steel bars. There was a crack and a shower of sparks and Cressy felt inordinately pleased at the little display of fireworks. She plucked a long, wet blade of grass from a clump at the bottom of the stone wall and held it against the gate. Not even a tingle. She dared to touch the gate and chuckled smugly to herself. If they thought it was that easy to get rid of Cressy Cross they were mistaken!

The only difficulty she had in climbing the gate was keeping hold of her camera. It didn't occur to her to pass it between the bars, and the strap kept getting hooked as she tried to lower herself over the top. She put it down to rest for a while when she reached the other side. She was trembling with exhaustion and unbearably hot again, and that made her madder than ever. The gate gave another little crackle where the bumper was still touching it. They must have fixed the fuse. Now Cressy was going to fix them!

By concentrating ruthlessly on the lighted rectangle of the front door Cressy made it up the long red gravel driveway. The house was huge and ugly, an old-fashioned jumble of white-painted timber with dormer windows sprouting all over the shingled roof. Spooky. Just the kind of house she would expect, from the unkind welcome it had given her! She lost a shoe on the way and her camera dropped out of her chilled hand into an ornamental garden but she didn't waver from her goal, even when two large, aggressive Alsatians bounded out of the darkness and set up a cacophony in her face. Animals she understood, better than people most times. These were well cared for and obviously well trained; threatening, warning, but making no move to attack. They would attack only by direct command. Cressy smiled at them kindly and at the big, bulky man who followed them out of the darkness and stared at her with an open mouth.

She didn't even get a chance to pound at the door. It was wrenched open as she aimed an unsteady finger at the bell-push. Her finger instead poked the chest of a tall brown man who stood in the doorway. Brown eyes, brown hair, brown skin and brown sports jacket and trousers. A brown bear. Cressy liked bears. She smiled at him.

'What in the——?'

'Uh—sorry, Mr Drake, the dogs just found her——'
The big man behind her quietened his charges as he found
his voice.

'Where? Is there a bordello in the grounds I don't
know about?' The bear had a brown voice, too, slightly
roughened by an Australian drawl. Weren't koalas grey?

'Do you own this house?' she rasped carefully.

'No...' The word came involuntarily as brown eyes
travelled disbelievingly over her, noting the one shoe,
the dark purple satin slathered against a small but lush
female body. Big eyes, the same dark cinnamon as the
widow's peak that accentuated the sweetheart face. Tiny
mouth, a cupid's bow. Flushed skin, slicked with
wetness.

'I'm here to see the person who *does*.' Cressy took
advantage of his abstraction to push past him, into the
brightly lit entryway.

The bear recovered a semblance of authority and
stiffened. 'Briscoe, where in the hell did she come from?'

'I don't know, Mr Drake——'

'Well, find out. See if there's anyone else in the
grounds. Get Chambers to cover the other side of the
house.' He snapped his fingers impatiently. 'Well, go
on, don't just stand there drooling!'

'Uh, sure, Mr Drake.'

Cressy was already heading down the hallway towards
the back of the house, leaving damp footprints on the
polished wood floor.

'Now, just a moment, Miss Whoever-you-are—you
can't just walk in here and——'

'I know. It took a *great deal* of trouble for me to get
here.' Cressy scowled, forced to halt as the bear shambled
in front of her. 'Where is he?'

'Who?'

'You know who,' she said cunningly, hoping he would
tell her.

'No, I don't, why don't you come along with me and tell me all about it . . . ?'

Cressy was trying not to show how confused she was. Everything was very hazy except for the certain knowledge that there was a dangerous killer loose probably down that hall where the bear didn't want her to go.

'OK,' she said, beaming at him to show there were no hard feelings, tucking her arm lightly through his.

'Maybe we can find you something to wear while we talk,' he said, relaxing slightly. 'You must be freezing.'

'Sure.' She patted his arm and turned with him. But where he ended up facing the other direction Cressy did a one-hundred-and-eighty-degree turn and shot off in her original direction.

'Hey——!'

She burst through the double doors at the end of the long hallway and stopped dead. The large room was almost filled by a huge table and around it sat a number of men. Hard men, tough men, middle-aged bullies dressed in suits and puffing cigars. Cressy had seen scenes just like this in gangster movies.

The murmur of conversation died instantly at the sight of her. Cressy recovered from the shock first. Her eyes swept around the perimeter of the table. In her feverish state they all looked the same—big, slit-eyed, mean. Except the man at the far end. He was small, and quite a bit younger than the rest, and her gaze nearly skimmed dismissively past him until she saw his eyes. They were silver, the colour of tensile steel or diamonds of the first water. The colour of power. She knew instinctively that she had found her quarry.

She pointed. 'You——!'

He took a moment to respond to her hoarse command, and in that moment the angry bear caught up with her.

'Sorry, Dev——'

A wave of a hand stopped him. The man straightened in his chair and Cressy realised that his smallness had been an illusion; he had only been slumping in his chair. Now he unwound himself and stood up. Not tall but definitely not small, not in any way. 'Me?'

Somehow she got the impression that beneath his shock was a wary amusement. He thought killing people was a joke!

'What is this? A half-opened strip-o-gram?' he asked. It got an uncertain laugh from some of his mobsters.

'I know what you're trying to do!' she accused hoarsely.

His amusement faded abruptly. Hah! She had him worried now! 'Oh, yes, I know exactly what you're up to and I'm not going to let you get away with it!'

'No?' With a single glance the man had quelled the mutter that rose around the table. He came towards her, through the smoke-laden air. Prowled would be a better word. Like a black panther, not expending an ounce of unnecessary energy to stalk his prey. His body was lithe and compact inside the dark conventional clothes, his black hair cut uncompromisingly short and streaked with ice, and an uncompromising face to match, its aquiline bone-structure contradicted by a harsh, unaristocratic toughness in the angle and curve of his features. A hairline scar ran from the corner of his left eye to the back of his jaw, like a long silver scratch against the olive skin.

Scratch. Claws. Cressy shivered. She had bad memories of a black panther. No malice had been intended, the animal had merely been acting true to its nature. To hunt, to kill, to protect their young... these were instinctive impulses and to get in the way of any of them was asking for trouble.

'What am I not going to get away with?' asked the panther, so close now she could scent the danger in him, hot and musky. The silver eyes, though, they weren't right somehow, not for a panther. They were the colour of summer lightning, like the electric blue-white crackle on the gate.

'Murderer!' she spat. 'I know what you're plotting and planning is all about, and I'm going to tell everyone. Everyone!' Her voice had risen to a painful, whispered shout as she threatened him fiercely, 'You thought you could keep me out, but I know all your secrets and I'm going to use them to see that you get what you deserve——'

A soft curse cut across the wild words bubbling out of her mouth. She heard the panther's growl, something about 'another damned fanatic'.

'You're the one who's damned, not me! Murderer!' She taunted him with her knowledge. 'How many lives have you notched on your gun barrel so far?'

He flinched and she laughed again. Her head whirled and the world turned over and she felt the bear prop her up as snatches of muttered conversation sank into her soggy brain.

'...crazy...must be on something...'

'...did she get in...? Had to have had help...'

'...got to get rid of her...'

They meant to kill her and dump her body! She found her sea-legs and staggered out into the hallway, only to lose her sense of direction and blunder back into a hard chest. Dimly she heard a door slam, cutting off the rumbling masculine speculation in the room she had just left.

Cressy tried to shake off the muscular shackles she knew belonged to the dark predator. The cylinder of film dropped out of her slip and was scooped up from the floor by a brown paw.

'Devil—she's carrying *film*.'

The shackles locked dizzyingly tight over her chest as another voice cut across the distressing buzzing in her ears.

'Found out why the power surged, Mr Connell. They temporarily shorted out the gates with some metal. And I found these.' It was the guard from outside, and 'these' were her camera and her shoe. Cressy made a clumsy swipe at them and a curse seared her hot ear.

'Is this your camera?'

She hung between his hands, exhausted.

'I said, is the camera yours?' He gave her a shake that made her head and stomach reel in tandem.

'Of course it is, give it back.' She made another futile lunge and glared at her angry captor. 'So now you're a thief, as well as a murderer!'

'I wouldn't throw stones if I were you. How did you get in here? Why did you take off your clothes? Were you supposed to be a diversion? Are you an activist or a journalist? Who are you working for?'

His avalanche of questions almost buried her, but one word made a connection in her fevered brain and she grabbed at it gratefully.

'Journalist...?' Journalists worked for newspapers. *She* was working for a newspaper! And it needed her photographs as soon as possible. She had promised. 'Gotta go——'

His grip tightened. 'You're not going anywhere until I know everything. Which paper do you work for?'

His eyes were icy. Maybe *they* could cool her down, maybe she could float away in their exquisitely chilly depths. In fact his whole body seemed beautifully cold and hard, but his clothes got in the way. They were scratchy, hurting her sensitised skin. She pushed aside his jacket and began to unbutton his shirt.

'What the——?'

'Seems she likes you, Devil,' an amused voice commented.

Cressy squinted sideways. The bear. No, not a bear...some kind of bird, that was what the guard had called him. It had been an aquatic bird. She brightened, remembering. 'Mr Duck!'

He laughed. 'Something like that! And you're Cinderella, right?'

'Frank, this isn't a bloody social occasion——'

'She's high as a kite, Devil. You're not going to get any sense out of her now. If she's a reporter she's certainly in no state to file a story tonight.'

Cressy had bared a little patch of chest. It was covered with thick, dark, silver-streaked hair like that on his head. A panther's pelt. In spite of her aversion to the beast Cressy laid her cheek against the exposed flesh and felt the muscular recoil as he swore again.

The hand that was biting into her right shoulder splayed out, then slid up to the nape of her neck. 'My God, she's hot; she's burning up! What the hell is she doing wandering about half naked?'

Cressy rubbed her face into his cool skin. 'Of course I'm burning up, you tried to fry me,' she wavered.

The hand wound around her sopping tail of hair and pulled her head back. A grim face studied her huge, glitteringly drugged eyes and the sheen of moisture on her face contrasting with the shiny dryness of her small mouth.

'She's not high, she's ill,' he realised, cupping her face to confirm his diagnosis. His hand was slightly callused, abrasively cool and pleasantly dry. He sounded angry but Cressy didn't care, as long as he kept his hand there.

'Mmm, nice...' she murmured, closing her eyes, turning her mouth into his scarred palm, licking it.

He made a strangled sound and whipped it away. Her head flopped like a blossom on a broken stem.

'What the hell are we going to do with her?' he exploded.

'Get a doctor would be the first thing.'

Devlin Connell looked down at the woman in his arms. She was as limp as a dishrag and it was impossible to see her as any kind of threat right now, except a passive one. He shrugged. He had no choice. 'Call Chester. And then go back in there and smooth things over. I'll take her upstairs——'

'They're going to want to know what's going on. Who she is and why she's here when they were told not to bring any of their own people,' Frank Drake pointed out.

'Stall until *we* find out. Use whatever that works. Put it all on to me. Imply there's a personal relationship involved, that'll cover a lot of bases.'

Frank Drake grinned. 'Judging by the way she's trying to crawl into your shirt it may not be a lie!'

'She's sick. I doubt if she knows what the hell she's doing. Or saying,' Devlin said impatiently. He swung her up into his arms. 'If Chester can't come right away, get him to phone me. I don't know what her temperature is, but it's sky-high. If we have to get her to hospital we may as well be prepared in advance. And see if you can find her damned clothes!'

Cressy, who was drifting nicely, was jolted out of her catatonia by this new form of bondage.

'What are you doing?' she slurred, staring up at his grim face.

'Taking you upstairs to bed.'

She came to sluggish life. 'Let me go, you . . . you lecherous pig!'

He controlled her easily. 'You should be so lucky,' he murmured acidly. He had noticed, even in the midst of the shock of her appearance at what was supposed to be a highly secret gathering, that she wasn't his type. Her charms were too obviously abundant, her body almost bursting out of that paper-thin wet slip. A woman of her height should be slim and delicately proportioned.

'I know what you want to do. You want to get rid of me!'

'Too true. Unfortunately, it's out of the question at the moment.'

'People know where I am, you know,' she warned him, licking her hot lips, keeping a wary eye on the high wood-panelled ceiling which was creeping suffocatingly down towards her.

'What people?'

Unfortunately she couldn't quite remember. Now the ceiling was going sideways, she noted in alarm. 'Where are you taking me?' She had forgotten that, too.

'To bed.' He tucked her on one hip as he opened a door and then he was setting her down on her uncertain feet. 'Who knows where you are?' he asked again, turning her face towards him.

'Where am I?' Cressy was bewildered.

The breath hissed between his teeth. 'What's your editor's name?'

'Shaw.' It just came out, without conscious thought. The scar on his face seemed to shimmer and she lifted a heavy hand to touch it. Her wounded panther. 'Did something fight back?'

He pushed her hand away. 'You could say that. What's your name?'

'I don't care.' Cressy found herself sinking back on to the broad, low bed that pushed itself into the back of her knees. It was so cool, the polished cotton of the quilt blissfully smooth to her painful touch.

'I do. What's your name?' he insisted, bending over her, cool hands on her.

'Are you going to kill me?' she murmured dreamily, thinking it might be a relief.

'The temptation is considerable,' he replied drily.

'Devil...' It was a dry whisper on her lips.

'Mmm?' He was noting her rapid pulse, her wrist lying trustingly in his hand.

'He called you a devil. Is that where I am? Am I dead and gone to hell? Is that why this room is all red?' With a burst of energy she said crossly, 'It's not a very soothing colour, you know.'

'This room wasn't designed to soothe. Don't worry, you're not dead yet, but you might be if we don't get these wet things off you and your fever down. What name should I put on the tombstone, just in case?'

Cressy knew of a name that deserved a decent burial. It was a professional name that she was proud of, but one she had outgrown and didn't use any more. He was kind, offering to do it for her.

'Kerr.'

'Kerr what? Or what Kerr?'

She could feel the hot breath of the panther on her face, see the excitement in the silver eyes. His teeth were white, strong... very close to her throat. He was a very polite panther, she realised. He had to know her name before he sank his fangs into his victim. If she didn't tell him he couldn't tear at her. Her little mouth pressed shut. Her eyes too.

He said other things, the panther. None of them made much sense to her so she didn't even try to reply. She had other things to worry about. Pains were shooting through her limbs, the red room was stifling, and giant insects were crawling over her, plucking at her slip. She sobbed in fear and tried to slap them away and heard a throaty growl. She lifted her painfully weighted lids and saw it was the panther man. He was rolling her slip off her hips and reaching for the front clasp of her saturated bra. He couldn't eat her, so the beast was going to rape her!

'Pervert!' she gasped wretchedly, clawing weakly at his hands as he released her breasts. Tears began rolling down her cheeks, but they were hot, too, and gave her no ease. They only made the predatory face hovering above her blurry and more frighteningly indistinct in the red mist.

Then something moist and cold was on her face, sponging away the sweat and tears, and the panther was growling again, but it was a soft and soothing growl, not the hungry snarl of a ravening beast. The coolness transferred to her shoulders and chest, across her breasts and stomach to her aching thighs. But it was only a momentary, drifting chill that was soon swallowed up again in the raging inferno inside her. She thrashed and fought to escape from it, to no avail. She clung to the one certainty in her confusion. It was all his fault, that...that *thing* that had attacked her outside in the rain with sharp needles of pain, cornered and captured her and dragged her off to his evil blood-drenched lair to toy with her at his leisure. With the last of her strength she was going to make damned sure he knew whom she held responsible!

Devlin stared at the doctor in outrage but the bluff, weathered young man ignored his scowl with the ease of long friendship.

'Why does she have to stay here? I have a helicopter out there. Why don't we just fly her to Waikato Hospital?' he growled, ignoring the thunder and lightning that was now playing outside.

'As I told you, her condition needs to be monitored but she's not in any immediate danger,' said Chester Grove, walking briskly to the stairs. 'I doubt the hospital would appreciate being bothered with what is just a simple viral illness. Give her plenty of liquids and those tablets and the tepid sponges and her temperature should come down within the next twenty-four hours. I'll call again in the morning to check up on her, but otherwise it's nothing you can't handle yourself.'

'But I don't even know the woman!' Devlin exploded in frustration.

However once Chester Grove had gone and Frank began to mount the stairs Devlin stopped him.

'Where in the hell are you going?'

'The doc said for someone to keep an eye on her until the fever breaks,' said Frank cheerfully.

'I'll do it,' Devlin bit out. 'You tell Seiver to serve dinner early and then sit in on the rest of the meeting. And I want to know as soon as security finds out anything——'

'But you said——'

'I know what I said. But you told them she was a very close personal friend of mine convalescing from a severe illness. It would seem suspicious if I didn't appear to worry about a relapse. They're skittish enough without having to worry about whether some unstable woman might take it into her head to get even with her callous swine of a lover by blowing the gaff. The world is full of unfortunates who underestimated the vindictiveness of a woman scorned. I'd rather be ridiculed for a mooning lover than have them suspect that she's a potential leak. And if they find out that she's a journalist we can kiss goodbye to their trust . . .'

Upstairs, fending off the flailing arms and legs of the frenzied woman, wincing as she landed a blow across his cheek, Devlin admitted to himself that logic had not been the only reason he had chosen to do this. He might have fiercely resisted the idea of having to succour an enemy, but he was damned if he was going to allow Frank to see her like this, so defenceless, and so . . . *naked*. In the circumstances, and considering the brazen method of her gatecrashing, the extent of his protectiveness surprised him, but, even sweat-soaked and delirious and fighting his help every step of the way, she was still a woman, and the thought of anyone else except Chester violating her physical privacy by the intimate handling of her helpless body was distasteful. Since he had already seen everything there was to see when he had stripped her, there was little point in pretending that she had any modesty left where *he* was concerned, but at least he could preserve some of her dignity by ensuring that the only strange eyes and hands that were laid upon her were his.

Still, he was a man, not a doctor, and it was impossible not to notice that her skin beneath his fingers was like hot silk pulled tautly over an exquisite softness, or that her breasts weren't quite as generous as the lacy bra had implied or that her hips were broad but not fleshy, their femininity enhanced by the rolling padded curves.

He noticed these things with a semi-dispassionate curiosity that he was rather proud of until he caught himself speculating whether he had been missing something all these years by preferring women who were slender and athletic and firmly muscled to a woman that a man could sink slowly, sensuously, deeply into...

He plunged the sponge and both his hands into the basin of tepid water at the bedside, cursing himself for the lapse in self-discipline. Even practically unconscious, the woman was a troublemaker.

He had a feeling that, conscious, she was going to be a hell of a lot more!

CHAPTER TWO

CRESSY blinked at the billowing red satin above her. She shifted her head and winced at the throbbing the movement invoked. It eased after a moment and she rolled from her back to her side, marvelling at the amount of effort it took.

The room before her steadied and she let out a weak, whispery laugh. It was furnished in atrociously bad taste, a kind of rococo nightmare, all plush red and garish gold. The wallpaper was a flocked red and gold, the carpet was the same shade of deep red as the satin fabric ceiling and the furniture gilt and velvet-upholstered mock-antique. Even the bed in which she was lying was an offence to the eyes, gilt cherubs and swans and crowns rising over the heart-shaped red buttoned headboard. And on the wall behind her she discovered a huge mirror, its gold frame bulging with carved fruits reflecting the entire room in all its vulgar glory.

Slowly, carefully, Cressy sat up and leaned gratefully back against the cushioned headboard. The gold silk sheets slid to her waist and she frowned at the sight of the soft, well-worn blue T-shirt that fell in generous folds around her body. Vague fancies danced in her head. Muddled thoughts of haunting, taunting devils. She pressed a hand to the aching nape of her neck and winced when her fingers brushed in the crusty plait. Where was she? Who——?

The door to the room whipped open and Cressy clutched the sheet to her chest, and then relaxed slightly as she stared at the man who strode in, balancing a small tray on one stubby hand. He was short and barrel-chested, his iron-grey hair a bristly crew-cut, his blue eyes piercing in a ruggedly ugly face. He was well into middle-age, Cressy guessed, but walked with a spring that defied his age. He wore a black shirt with rolled-up sleeves and the muscles on his tattooed arms were hard and ropy.

'Thought you'd be waking up soon. Thirsty?' He put the tray down on a disgusting little bedside table and Cressy saw a crystal jug filled with yellow juice.

'Yes.' It took two attempts to get her throat moving. 'Thanks...' She drank, easing the dryness in her throat. 'Er—who are you?'

'Seiver. And you're Kerr. Or is it Keir?' He spoke in a familiar rolling Irish burr.

Cressy ignored the opening. First things first. 'Where am I?'

A mirthless smile flickered across narrow lips. 'You've been asking that fifty times a day for the past two days.'

Two *days*? The last thing she could clearly remember was driving her car. 'Why? Haven't I been getting an answer?' she croaked suspiciously. The glass was heavy in her hand, so Cressy quickly finished the drink and put it down.

'Sure. But you never remembered it from one moment to the next.'

Vaguely Cressy began to form a memory and it wasn't a reassuring one. A smoky room, wall to wall in mobsters.

'So, where am I?'

'Rush House. Three Mile Junction.'

No wonder it hadn't registered. It didn't mean a thing. 'Who brought me here?' she said cautiously, testingly. 'Have *you* been looking after me?'

The man scowled as if she had insulted him. 'Not likely. It's the Devil himself been watching you.' His accent and phrasing was very like her father's, whose lilt was still strong despite the fact that he hadn't lived in Ireland for over fifty years.

'You mean, the devil looks after his own?' she re-edited his paraphrase, annoyed that a total stranger should judge her on the evidence of some apparently fevered ravings.

That brought forth a short, barking laugh. 'Oh, he does that, indeed he does.'

'I must have been pretty sick,' said Cressy, putting a hand to her throat. It still hurt and her skin still felt overly warm but her mind was rapidly clearing.

The man took her literally, informing her with unnecessary relish, 'More than once, and not quiet about it either.' He watched her push herself further upright, and grunted reluctantly, 'What d'ya think you're trying to prove? No point in getting up just to fall over. The doc said not to for a few days yet.'

'I don't remember a doctor,' Cressy said, discovering that his advice was well-founded.

Another laugh. 'Well, he'll be remembering you for a while. Didn't you give him a black eye, and he only trying to examine you!'

'I didn't!' breathed Cressy, all too afraid it was true. She was clumsy enough when she was in full command of her faculties; it didn't surprise her that she should be even worse when she was too ill to care to exercise them. 'Is he all right?'

'Apart from the damage to his digestive system. Had to eat his words, you see. Teased the Devil that he couldn't control an itty-bitty little thing like you. Then what happens? He looks to check you over and you haul off and belt him one. Fell on the floor, he did. And didn't the Devil laugh! Said every scratch and bite was worth it seeing the doc unseated.'

'Scratch and bite?' Had she wandered into an insane asylum, or a secret coven of devil worshippers?

'Ah, well, you didn't take kindly to being looked after. Not one to give in easily.' He sounded grudgingly respectful, but Cressy was horrified.

'I didn't bite you, did I?' It was a wonder she hadn't broken a tooth. His hide would be tough as old boots.

'He wouldn't let me near you when you were at your worst—wouldn't let anyone, except the doc.'

'He who?' demanded Cressy impatiently.

'I told you. Devil.'

Now Cressy was sure that she was being held in a madhouse . . . or a whorehouse, she thought hysterically, her eyes flickering around the scarlet room. Seiver spoke with every indication of sincerity, calmly, as if he really believed in the physical manifestation of evil.

'Now, you take one of these.'

Cressy stared at the pill that she was being offered. Weak as she was, she had to get out of here. Who knew what was in the pill? They might be keeping her drugged so that she couldn't escape to tell her tale.

'No, thanks. I'm feeling a lot better,' she lied.

She pushed the bedclothes back and swung her feet off the bed on to the floor, only just catching herself as the rest of her body threatened to follow suit.

'If you don't take it I'll get Devil to give it to you. He's been shovelling them down your throat every four hours for the last couple of days, rabies notwithstanding.'

Oh, had he indeed? Cressy remembered now, at least she thought she did. Hazy recollections of big hands touching her, hurting her, forcing her to do things she didn't want to do.

Doggedly Cressy stood up. Seiver made no further attempt to dissuade her. He folded his thick arms across his broad chest and watched with a sneer that only made Cressy more determined.

'See? I'm fine,' she insisted. 'Where are my clothes?'

'No idea, missy.'

'What do you mean, no idea? Where are the clothes I came in?' she demanded shrilly.

He showed some teeth. 'You mean that frilly stuff? Ain't been washed yet. I'm not in the laundering business, ya know. I'm just here to cook and clean rooms.'

Frilly stuff? Cressy closed her eyes, swaying, colour running up under her skin as she remembered. She had taken off the clothes in her car, and then locked them in. 'They're in my car.'

'What car? Ain't been no car found around here. We figured you'd been dropped off.'

Of course he'd say that if they wanted to trap her here. Cressy opened her eyes and glared at him. If that was the way they wanted to play it...

'I'll just wear this T-shirt, then. It covers more of me than my slip did, anyway. I'll find my car myself, thanks.'

'You ain't going nowhere, Kerr.' There was a ring of command in the gravelly voice. Ex-army? He had the build and the manner for it. Or maybe it was mob discipline that made him so tough. Strangely, the thought didn't frighten her as it should have.

'Says who?' Cressy said, in equally determined tones. She felt light and hollow. She wouldn't have to walk through him, she could fly over him! She laughed at his expression. He thought she was mad, but he was the one who was crazy! 'Put 'em up, Buster. Let's see if you're as tough as you make out!' She presented him with her fists. Unfortunately that overset her balance again, and as she staggered to right herself a windmilling fist struck his crooked nose. He yelled, and clapped his hand over his face. A bright red trickle of blood leaked between his fingers.

Cressy almost burst into tears of remorse. 'Oh, I'm sorry, are you OK? Let me see?' She put up a hand to pull away his and he jumped backwards.

'Keep away from me, you she-devil!' he howled. 'I ain't ever hit a woman yet but I'm thinking on it!'

Poor man. Totally deranged. He had devils on the brain. Cressy was swept with a wave of compassion. 'I didn't mean to hit you. I think I'm still a bit light-headed. Look, if you help me get out of here, you can come with me. I can take you somewhere the devil can't reach——' She paused hopefully but Seiver just stood there, mopping up the blood with a tissue from the bedside drawer, staring sourly over her shoulder.

'Tell her, Seiver. Tell her there's nowhere the Devil can't reach if he has a mind to.'

The black velvet voice, gilded with a grim amusement, sent horror trickling down Cressy's spine. For a moment she didn't dare turn around to see what manner of being had hypnotised Seiver. She had to force herself, summoning all her defensive scepticism, turning carefully to make sure she didn't disturb her fragile balance.

No horns, no hoofs, no pitchfork. Those were the first things that she noticed to her inexpressible relief. Just a man. Her eyes rose to his and it was like a blow of recognition. This was Him, the one they called Devil. The chief mobster, the man she had fought in her delirium. She looked at his hands. They were disproportionately large for his size, strong, hard, callused hands, the fingers blunt, and slightly irregular. She shivered.

'Cold? You must be on the mend,' the velvet murmur continued. 'Why don't you get back into bed?'

Cressy's hands bunched. 'I'm leaving!'

'She popped me one when I tried to stop her,' Seiver complained, displaying the damage.

'You can't say you weren't warned, Seiver. Are you going to get back into that bed, Kerr? Or am I going to have to put you there?'

'Don't you touch me!' Cressy swayed warningly.

'It's a bit late for that, sugar——'

'Don't try your sweet talk on me!' Cressy sought wildly for a defence. 'Maybe you're hoping I wouldn't remember what I stumbled into downstairs, but I do...'

The silver eyes narrowed. 'Are you saying that it was just coincidence you're here?'

Not sure what he was talking about, Cressy neither confirmed nor denied it. She was battling a dizzy feeling again, but was grimly determined not to wilt under that penetrating stare. Maybe it would be politic to be pleasant. She swallowed, uncomfortably aware of her parched, painful throat.

'Look, Mr...'

'Connell,' he supplied cynically, his scepticism of her ignorance writ large on the arrogant, aggressive face. 'Devlin Connell.'

The rush of relief at finding such an innocuous reason for his nickname overwhelmed a faint echo of remembrance. 'So that's why they call you "Devil".'

He tilted his head slightly, and the silvery scar caught the light from the old-fashioned sash-window on the far side of the room. 'If it reassures you to think so,' he said smoothly, sending another *frisson* down her back. He had known exactly what she was thinking.

'Mr Connell, I appreciate you taking care of me when I was sick, but I'm better now and it's time I was on my way.'

'Where?'

'What?'

'Where were you going?'

Why did he want to know? 'Coromandel,' she said warily.

He acknowledged her evasiveness with the lift of his eyebrow, which pulled at the scar. 'From where?'

'Auckland.'

'Hitch-hiking? Is that how you lost your clothes? Some kind motorist try to take advantage of your criminal irresponsibility?'

'I wasn't hitching, I was driving. I'm not an idiot, you know!' Cressy rasped furiously.

'No, indeed. I never thought you were. In fact, you're a clever woman. A very clever woman.' He took a single step towards her. It was enough. Cressy took three wobbly steps back, hard against the bed. 'What were you after when you came here?'

'Strange as it may seem, help. My car ran into a ditch down the road. I almost killed myself on your gate, you know.'

He showed not an ounce of remorse. 'The charge isn't lethal; that would be illegal.'

'You would know,' Cressy muttered, then wished she hadn't when he moved closer, bending to catch what she said. She recognised his scent . . . the scent of danger.

'Why do you say that?'

'Look. All I want are my clothes, which are in my car, and a tow out of the ditch, then I'll be on my way,' she blustered. If she didn't sit down in a moment she was going to faint.

'I'll bet you will. And no doubt you want your camera back, too.'

More memories swam to the surface. 'Of course I do,' she snapped.

He studied her consideringly. 'You're fighting a losing battle, you know. Why don't you lie down before you fall down?'

'I don't feel like lying down!'

He sighed. The blunt tip of his forefinger pressed against her breastbone and exerted the merest pressure. Cressy went down like a felled log, sprawling across the bed. Seiver snickered.

'She wouldn't take her pill, either.' He picked it up from the floor and tossed it over to his boss.

'I don't approve of unnecessary medication,' Cressy's husky snarl didn't carry much bite as she doggedly gathered her limbs together and sat up.

'Believe me, this is very necessary. If you don't finish the antibiotics you'll probably have a relapse which will be more virulent than the first time. Or is being helpless and bedridden all part of the scenario?'

'It's an antibiotic?' Cressy took the tablet and squinted at the well-known brand name embossed on the white surface. 'Let me see the bottle.'

'Mistrustful little thing, aren't you?' He handed her the bottle. 'But I suppose in your profession it's considered healthy.'

'My profession?' Why should a wildlife photographer need to cultivate distrust?'

'Journalist. That's what you told us you were.'

'Did I?' If Cressy's mind could have raced, it would have. As it was it could only manage a slow jog. If only she could remember the details of their first encounter.

'Mmm. And that's odd. Because there's no woman named Kerr registered with the New Zealand Journalists' Union. There is a man called Kerr associated with the Environmental Action Group, though. No relation, I suppose?'

Cressy was instantly alerted by the overt casualness, and the fact that this man had bothered to try and find out about her. She knew Bill Kerr but she didn't approve of the EAG's methods, even though she approved of their ultimate goal—peaceful co-existence with the natural environment.

'None at all.' She evaded his penetrating stare by filling her glass with more juice and washing down the pill. She put down the glass and paused, half expecting to keel over.

'What did you think it was? A knockout pill?' Devlin Connell asked drily, watching her mentally monitor her internal processes. 'You'd better go down and see to lunch, Seiver. The natives are getting restless.'

'What else should I think? He——' a nod at the smugly retreating Seiver '—didn't tell me what it was. He kept raving on about devils. A remote house in the middle of nowhere...electrified gates...guards...sinister inhabitants. I could have been in line for sacrifice at a black mass...'

'Only if you're a virgin. Is that why you're so anxious to leave?'

'You mean you don't know?' Cressy snarled to cover her humiliation. 'You certainly pawed me enough.'

'And I have the scars to prove it.' He turned his head and Cressy found herself staring at the fresh scratches on the side of his neck. 'I've got several strategic bruises, too, if you'd care to reassure yourself that you successfully defended your virtue in the time-honoured female fashion.' His hand went to the tooled leather belt at his hips and Cressy blushed.

Her eyes were the colour of ground black pepper as she asked bitterly, 'Why did *you* have to look after me?'

'Because there are no women here and as the owner I felt you were my responsibility.'

'You hurt me,' she accused him. 'I remember fighting you.'

He sat down on the bed, the depression on the mattress tipping her cross-legged figure towards him.

'It was the illness you were fighting, not me. You were drenched and almost totally delirious by the time you got to the house. As far as you were concerned everyone was your mortal enemy, out to stop you doing whatever it was you thought you had to do. It was either forcibly restrain you or let you commit suicide by rushing back out into the storm. The drugs alone couldn't bring your temperature down. You had to be bathed in cool water every half-hour for the better part of twenty-four hours before the fever broke.'

'You mean the doctor stayed all that time?' Cressy groaned, thinking of the bill. She made a great deal of money in her specialised field but, because the travel expenses were high, she never seemed to save very much.

'Not the doctor. Me.'

What she had thought was a blush before had only been a mild rash in comparison to what happened now. Cressy rolled away from him and buried her hot face in the red pillow. She knew he had undressed her initially, but this...! Not even the knowledge of what he had saved her on doctor's bills was a comfort!

There was silence in the big room. Cressy's embarrassment began to slide into annoyance. The least he could do was apologise, or utter something reassuring about how it had all been utterly clinical. She lifted her head from the pillow and eyed his bland face.

'I'm sorry I was a bother,' she growled, trying to elicit the required response.

'Oh, you were. An awful bother. But I rather enjoyed having you at my mercy after the way you burst in here.'

Definitely *not* reassuring. The sliver of amusement in his pale eyes told her he knew what she had expected and was deliberately prolonging her embarrassment.

'That wasn't entirely my fault. I told you, my rental car broke down and then your gates attacked me——'

'Strange, then, that we haven't been able to find any sign of a car within a radius of five kilometres, and I don't believe that in your condition you could have walked any further.'

This was too much like an interrogation for Cressy's liking. In the circumstances he probably had every right to be suspicious, but he was acting pretty suspiciously himself for a man with nothing to hide. 'Look, my car must have been stolen. I locked the keys in it by mistake. All they'd have to do was get in and they wouldn't even have had to hot-wire it!'

'I doubt there's been a car theft in this area for years.'

'There's a first time for everything.' Cressy wasn't used to being disbelieved. 'And my car would have been tempting. There was a lot of equipment in there——

photographic equipment. And my bag with all my money and credit cards——'

'And your ID. How convenient...'

'This isn't a police state, you know. One doesn't have to carry pass-books around——'

'True, but common courtesy should dictate an introduction. I gave you my name but I doubt that Kerr is really yours.'

'It's my professional name. Cressida Kerr. I'm a photographer——'

'You said you were a journalist.'

'Did I?' She shrugged. 'Photo-journalist, then.' It was barely true. Although she took detailed notes on location, it was usually someone else who whipped them into shape for publication. Cressy was an acknowledged expert in the photographic study of rare and endangered species but even she would admit she was no writer.

'On a particular assignment?'

'I'm working for a paper at the moment, yes.'

'Which one?'

'Why do you want to know?'

'Why don't you want me to know?'

'Oh, for goodness' sake!' Cressy flopped backwards on the bed, her head spinning all over again. Bitter experience had taught her to be cagey when people tried to find out the exact location of some of her photographic expeditions. Sometimes the continued survival of a species depended on her discretion. Not in this case, of course, but still... 'I feel terrible.'

'That's because you haven't eaten. And because you don't want to answer any more questions,' he said drily.

'I'm surprised you didn't try to ferret everything out of me while I was delirious,' Cressy snapped.

'I did,' he admitted coolly.

Cressy eyed him cautiously, sensing more humiliation in store. 'What did I say?'

He didn't disappoint her. 'Some of it I wouldn't sully your ears by repeating, some of it was nonsense and a lot of it appeared to be fantasy, erotic and otherwise,' he told her in that taunting velvety drawl. 'Quite a lot of the time you seemed fixated on the idea that I was some kind of jungle animal and that I was going to do all sorts of deliciously terrible things to you if you let me.'

'It's a habit of mine, comparing people to animals,' Cressy muttered. 'I thought you looked like a black panther.'

'Strong and dark and dangerous,' he mused. 'If you're as perceptive when you're conscious as you are when you're semi-conscious I would say that you're a very clever journalist.'

'Photographer!' Cressy corrected him irritably. Was he warning her about himself, or threatening her?

'Whatever.' He shrugged easily. 'I definitely loomed large in your ravings...Cressida.' He tested the name on his tongue, as if tasting it for veracity.

'Cressy,' she sighed. Cressida had always been far too proper for her. And, since she had gone this far, 'Cressy Cross.'

'Cross?' Suspicion flared anew in the silver eyes.

'Kerr is my middle name. Look, Mr Connell, I don't know why you're so paranoid but you don't have to worry about me. I specialise in wildlife photography. I was on my way to Whitianga—to photograph some insects on Middle Island, the nature reserve.'

'Insects? *This* is the rush assignment? The vital job that I was stopping you from doing!'

She didn't blame him for sounding incredulous. A lot of people didn't think that insects loomed very large in the scheme of things, but Cressy found them every bit as complex and fascinating and worthy of study as higher species.

'Not just any insects,' she reproved him. 'Giant wetas—sort of big, carnivorous crickets. They're about ten centimetres long and can jump one and a half metres, and have tusks that they use for fighting or singing. They've just been rediscovered after about twenty years. The Conservation Department is launching a study. I'm doing a photo-essay on them for a newspaper, and a wildlife magazine...'

'I presume I can check all of this?'

'You can check all you damn well like!' Cressy told him furiously. 'But don't expect me to hang around for vindication. I have a deadline and I've already lost two days——'

'And you'll have to lose a few more. You can hardly stand on your feet, let alone walk downstairs. And what about your equipment and your car?'

'You mean you really don't have it hidden away somewhere?' Cressy asked, hoping her suspicions had been right after all.

He held her eyes steadily as he shook his head and rose from the bed, thrusting his hands into his pockets. 'I wish it were so easy...' he murmured broodingly.

'I don't see what the difficulty is. I want to leave; you want to get rid of me. If we help each other out we'll both get what we want.'

'I wonder...'

His eyes strayed over her supine body and she wondered whether he was seeing her the way she had been over the past few days. Nervously she pulled at the hem of the big T-shirt to make sure it was well down over her thighs. 'Can't you get me some clothes, at least?'

'That T-shirt is the smallest I have, so I can't see any of my trousers fitting you. If your car isn't found you can give me your size and I'll send Seiver in to the Junction and buy you something.'

'What do you mean, *if*? Of course it'll be found. In fact, if you let me use a telephone I can report it to the police right away.'

'Give me the details, I'll report it for you. What rental company was it?'

'But they'll want to speak to *me*.'

'He, not they. There's only one country constable to cover the whole plains. James is a personal friend of mine. I doubt that he'll need to bother you as long as you give me sufficient information to pass on.'

'But I *want* to be bothered!' burst out Cressy in exasperation.

'The doctor said that you needed to take it very easy, no strains or upsets——'

'I suppose *he's* a personal friend of yours, too,' said Cressy sarcastically.

'As a matter of fact, yes.'

'Well, I still have to call my editor and explain why my pics are going to be late,' Cressy insisted.

'Give me his number and I'll call. If you're well enough to phone he might consider you should be well enough to meet your deadline.'

'I also have to notify the rental company about the car.'

'Let Seiver do that. He's paid to handle these tiresome hassles.'

It was very smoothly done, but suddenly Cressy realised what he was doing. 'You don't want to let me use the telephone, do you?'

'The telephones are all downstairs and the doctor said no strain, remember?'

'You could carry me.'

'In nothing but a T-shirt?'

'You're trying to stop me making a call. Even criminals get to make a call from prison. Is that what I am—a prisoner?'

'Only of your own ill-health.'

'Then why won't you let me use the telephone? What are you afraid of? It's something to do with me being connected with a newspaper, isn't it? You were paranoid when you thought I was a reporter. You thought I was here to write about you? What are you hiding?'

'I'm not hiding anything, I'm trying to stop you risking a relapse. But I can't force you to be sensible——'

'No, you can't. Any more than I can force you to be on the level.' She gasped as he swiftly bent over her and swept her up against his chest. 'What are you doing?'

'Taking you to a telephone. Isn't that what you want so badly?'

'I can walk,' she said feebly.

'You haven't eaten anything for more than three days. You're as weak as a kitten. For once, can you restrain your impulsiveness and accept help without fighting?'

'For once? You talk as if you know all about me. You didn't even know my name until a few minutes ago,' Cressy said stoutly. 'For your information, I'm usually very amenable, and not at all impulsive.'

'Really?' His murmur was disbelieving and Cressy glared up at his unrelenting jaw as he carried her out of the room.

'How did you get the scar?'

The tight line of his mouth eased into a wry curve. 'And you say you're not impulsive. Most people don't dare reveal such indelicate curiosity, not at the first meeting, anyhow.'

'This isn't our first meeting. As you were at pains to point out, we're already intimately acquainted,' Cressy said rashly. A mistake, since she made herself acutely aware of the way the muscles of his chest moved against her thinly clad side, and the way his hips swayed against the curve of her buttock as he walked. She reached up and touched the silvery line on his face, curiously tracing the soft cicatrice. He jerked his head away like a wounded animal. 'I'm sorry. Does it still hurt?'

'Not after ten years.'

Yet he didn't like it being touched. 'How did it happen?'

'You don't give up, do you? I was injured in a very isolated part of the world. It was several days before I could get to a doctor to get it stitched and in the meantime it got infected.'

'Was it a knife?' It went with her image of him.

'Violence isn't romantic, little one, and no, I'm sorry to disappoint you but it was nothing so glamorous as a knife. A sharp piece of metal. A mine caved in on me.'

Cressy made a soft sound of horror. 'Were you trapped?'

'Luckily, no. There was another entrance, although it took a while to find it, since it was pitch-black. I didn't know I'd been cut until I got outside and discovered what I thought was leachate saturating my shirt was actually blood. Your telephone, ma'am.'

So absorbed in his stark description had Cressy been that she hadn't noticed them entering another bedroom, this as spare and tasteful as hers was florid and tasteless. A big double bed and a desk and chair were almost the only furnishings, their warm wood complementing the cream walls and floor.

'This isn't downstairs!' she said, as he set her down by a polished rimu desk on which sat the latest in elaborate telecommunication systems. 'You said there weren't any phones up here.'

'I forgot,' he said blandly. He picked up the slim white telephone and punched in a couple of numbers. 'There, you have a line out.'

'Thank you. You don't have to stay,' said Cressy, restraining her snort with difficulty.

'It's no trouble,' he said, going around to sit in the curved rimu chair behind the desk, picking up some papers.

'I would like some privacy for my call,' Cressy said tartly, tucking the receiver under her chin.

'What if you feel faint?'

'I'll lie down. Now if you don't mind, Mr Connell...'

He allowed her a moment to think that he wasn't going to obey her command and wonder how she could hope to enforce it before he rose lazily.

'I'll be in the bathroom if you need me——' he sauntered towards the panel door on the far side of the bed, running a hand across his chin '—shaving. I felt your soft fingers snag on my beard and I'd hate to be the cause of chafing that lovely smooth, milky skin...'

As if he would get close enough! Cressy's finger was trembling a little as she punched in the *Star*'s number. Unfortunately the illustrations editor wasn't there, so Cressy had to explain to his deputy that her trip had been delayed by the loss of her rental car and equipment. He didn't seem to think there would be any problem slotting in the story later than planned, and after they had discussed a new deadline Cressy asked to be switched through to Nina, her flatmate, a staff photographer at the *Star*.

'Bower.'

'Nina. It's me. What do you think of when I mention the name Devlin Connell?' Cressy spoke low and rapidly into the phone, one eye on the closed bathroom door.

'Sex.'

'Nina, be serious!' Nina was always quick with a hard-edged joke. She was a big, bouncy blonde who had taken photographs purely as a hobby until her husband walked out on her, leaving her with a mountain of unpaid bills and a cynical view of life. Instead of letting it get her down, Nina had turned around and at the age of thirty-five built a career for herself out of her hobby by flooding papers and magazines with photographs taken on spec until one of them realised her untapped potential and took her on.

'OK. Money. Gold, silver, platinum...'

'Nina!'

'I'm telling you! He's heavily into mining. Owns quite
a few companies doing mineral and oil exploration. Inherited from Papa, a Kiwi roughneck who made a pile
wildcatting oil in the States about the time that oil for-
tunes were easy to win and lose, providing you had the
guts and nerve and weren't afraid to soil your hands.
Oh, and he's due to retire shortly.'

'Who? Papa?' Cressy could feel herself wilting, and
propped her hip against the edge of the desk.

'Oh, no, he retired a while ago. Bad health. Lives in
Spain and grows oranges or port or something...his wife
is Spanish——' that explained the devil-dark colouring
combined with the light eyes '—no, it's Devlin who's
due to retire.'

'Are you sure?' They couldn't be talking about the
same person. Was she being harboured by an impostor?

'If you weren't more interested in the mating habits
of the common housedog flea than what happens in the
real world, you wouldn't have to ask. He was a real arrogant so-and-so when he took over his father's oil
interests and announced that he had no intention of
letting the business break up his health the way it had
broken his father's. Said that he would make all the
money he would ever need in the shortest possible time
and retire to enjoy the proceeds before he was forty. He's
forty next year. He may wish he hadn't been so brash
back then, but no one's ever let him forget that claim,
least of all the Press. Every year on his birthday someone
does a story on him. The countdown is sort of an in-
joke in the business community——'

'Married?'

'Nah...nearly was once, though, to some sultry
señorita related through his mother's family, which is
pretty aristocratic, apparently. I can dig the dirt on him
if you want me to go look at the files. Why the interest?

Has he been doing something he shouldn't in your little corner of the world?'

Nina meant in the world of nature. Cressy was usually content with just taking pictures of endangered species, letting her photographs express her outrage in a way that her unskilled words never could, but occasionally she was moved by despair to take action.

'I don't know. Maybe.' She gave Nina very sketchy details of where she was and why, obliquely giving her the impression that she hadn't yet met the Devil in question. Why exactly she was being so cautious she didn't know, because although Nina was "Press" Cressy knew that she placed friendship before ambition and would never publish anything that a friend had told her in confidence. It was just that until she was sure of her facts Cressy didn't think it was fair to indulge in wild speculation.

'OK. Well, if you need anything else give me a buzz.'

Cressy arranged for Nina to fast-post her a few clothes, which she felt was a far more acceptable arrangement than letting Devlin buy some for her. That smacked of being compromised. If the Post Office lived up to its promises the package should arrive in a couple of days.

By the time she hung up Cressy could feel a dew of perspiration dotting her brow and her hands felt clammy. Who would have thought talking on the telephone would require such an effort? Maybe Devlin *had* only been solicitous in offering to make her calls...

The door to the bathroom opened and Devlin came strolling out. 'Finished?' He didn't really look any more clean-shaven than when he'd gone in to Cressy's heavy eyes, but perhaps he had one of those fancy new razors that left a fashionable stubble in its wake. She nodded.

'You look rotten,' he said baldly. 'Back to bed?' He picked her up and she managed only a plaintive protest this time.

'This is a much nicer room than mine. Why can't I stay here?'

'Because this is my room and I don't like sharing.'

No wonder he wasn't married! 'My room makes me feel nauseous. Why can't I have another bedroom? There must be tons. This is an enormous house.'

'Because they're all——'

'All what?' Cressy asked light-headedly.

'All temporarily out of commission,' he said smoothly.

Cressy opened her mouth to ask whether they were being redecorated, and then realised that there could be another reason. They might all be occupied. Perhaps the meeting that she hazily remembered gate-crashing was still going on. But if that mean-looking bunch weren't thugs but respectable business connections, why was Devlin so anxious to keep it secret?

'I don't like red,' she said sulkily.

'It does rather clash with your hair.'

'What's wrong with my hair?' Cressy bristled all over.

'Nothing. It just doesn't go with red,' he said soothingly. 'It's still got mud and twigs in it, I'm afraid, but I didn't like to wash it when you were so ill, or comb it out when your head was obviously already painful. You can have a shower tomorrow, when you've got some food inside you and I can trust you not to pass out. I'm sure your hair is very pretty when it's clean. At the moment it's a very nondescript mud-brown.'

Pretty wasn't the word that Cressy heard used very often in connection with her hair. 'Vibrant', 'startling', 'different' were usually the polite euphemisms people used to describe its relentless orange.

'How do you know that it clashes with red, then?' said Cressy sullenly, jealously studying the subdued sheen of his own dark head.

'Certainly not from what's on your *head*,' he murmured blandly.

The outraged, screaming silence that greeted his remark lasted much longer than the time it took for him to dump her furious, stiffened body back on the red rose eiderdown and walk, chuckling, out of the door.

CHAPTER THREE

CRESSY glared at the man in the kitchen.

'I was only trying to help,' she insisted.

Seiver scowled at her. 'Well, do me a favour, missy, stop trying to help. That's the second jug you've broken. If you keep helping we're not going to have any crockery left!'

'It slipped off the tray,' said Cressy defensively. It was obviously not an opportune moment to apologise for the vase in her room that she had inadvertently knocked to the floor. Her friends didn't call her 'Crash Cross' for nothing!

'You're not supposed to be down here, anyway,' Seiver pointed out nastily as he swept up the pieces of glass.

'The doctor said I could get up today and I'm not going to spend all my time cooped up in that awful room just because your bullying boss wants me well out of the way.'

Seiver didn't say anything. Like Frank Drake, whom Connell had arrogantly ordered to keep her company when she began to make short, tottering forays out of bed, he was remarkably close-mouthed about his employer. If it hadn't been for her call to Nina, Cressy would still have been in the dark as to Connell's identity. Now, two days later, she felt strong enough to reassert herself. She had seen the postal van from her window that morning and had rushed downstairs to intercept Seiver before he had time to sort through the mail. Sure enough there was a brown parcel addressed to her and she had pounced on it with an air of triumph. She wouldn't have put it past Connell to ransom her good behaviour against her clothes. He had made no move to purchase her the promised alternative to his baggy T-shirt, claiming she wasn't well enough to get up anyway. Now she could thumb her nose at his attempted manipulation.

Seiver continued to ignore her and Cressy dug her hands into the pockets of her jeans and mooched back upstairs. She only had Connell's word that the police hadn't yet found her car and that her beloved Olympus needed repairs, and she didn't trust him an inch.

She had already sneaked into Connell's room to use the telephone and discovered that some neat piece of technology was in use to prevent unauthorised outgoing calls. More positive action was obviously now required.

What would Max do? Cressy's father was a specialist at getting into and out of tricky situations. As a freelance photo-journalist, Max roamed the world's trouble-spots exposing the ugliness, the corruption, the cynical reality that revealed the truth behind the brassy propaganda of war. Exposés were his forte. He had passed on his red hair, and his affinity with a camera, to his daughter, but not his feckless love of danger. It had taken Cressy years of floundering in near-failure to find her own, more gentle *métier* of wildlife photography, but Max had never failed to encourage and believe in her.

There was no question about what he would advise now. Max hated to feel hemmed in, personally or professionally. He would tell her it was her duty to escape!

It proved relatively simple to get out of the house without being seen. Outside her window was a drainpipe which provided a convenient stepping-stone to the fire escape that wound down the back of the building. Once down, she scuttled from shrub to shrub, ducking around the back of what appeared to be stables before climbing through white-painted rails to reach the safety of a thicket of trees. From there she blundered on until she came to a vaguely familiar dry-stone wall.

It looked over six feet high but in her lucid state she knew it was no barrier. She had done plenty of rock-climbing in her time.

To her surprise her legs were trembling when she landed on the gravel road on the other side of the wall and she straightened them impatiently. She was *not* a sickly weakling. The doctor had said she was run-down but he didn't realise how fit and active she normally was. She was more resilient than most people. Besides, he was a friend of Connell's; why should she believe him?

Now. Which way? She squinted at the morning sky and decided her best bet was east, the direction of Thames. At least, she assumed Thames was east, since she only had a vague idea of where she was.

The gravel had deep wheel-furrows in it but Cressy was disappointed to discover that it was apparently little used. She had been walking for what seemed like hours, although her watch told her it was only forty minutes, and still there was no sight or sound of traffic. The road had to lead somewhere, she told herself stubbornly as she slogged along the dusty verge, grateful that Nina had included sneakers in her care parcel. Pity she hadn't also included a map! The trembling in her legs began again and a hollow formed in the pit of her stomach. She hadn't been very hungry the day before but, mindful of the need to regain her strength, she had choked down some soup and bread at lunchtime and scrambled eggs for dinner—served, of course, in solitary splendour on a tray in her room. This morning she had had a couple of slices of toast and a cup of tea, but she hadn't been able to manage the muesli and fruit and the poached egg. Why couldn't Seiver have made her pancakes or something else sweet and filling? Because he wanted her to suffer, that was why!

She was sweating now, too, and she pulled off her soft grey jumper and tied it around her waist, telling herself it was only to be expected that exercise generated heat. She undid two buttons of her crisp blue shirt and tried to believe she was doing fine but eventually she had to sit down on a roadside rock and rest. Her breath caught in her raw throat as she contemplated the unappealing prospect of another forty minutes of walking. She felt like bursting into weak tears at the thought. Her weary spine stiffened. Stubborn pride was another legacy from her father. Self-pity got you nowhere.

As if to herald her spirit she heard the sound of an engine. She jumped up from the rock, wincing as her ankle turned, and looked hopefully back along the road. A red pick-up appeared, as dusty as the road, over the rise that had just sorely tried her aching calf muscles. A jolly country farmer, if she was lucky, one of those happy folk content to do a good turn for a fellow human without asking too many awkward questions.

She waved hopefully and the driver jammed on his brakes, the pick-up sliding sideways slightly with the momentum. The door that was thrust open nearly hit her.

'I thought you said you weren't an idiot. Get in, Cressida.'

Her luck was definitely out! Devlin's big hands were clenched on the wheel, as if to restrain them from flying around her neck.

'This is a public road, you can't make me do anything,' said Cressy weakly.

His smile was mockingly grim. 'Wrong, Cressida. If you wanted the highway you're going in the wrong direction. This is an access road across *my* property, and I have the right to deal with trespassers as I see fit.'

Inwardly Cressy was cursing and stamping. 'There are laws——'

'Since when is the Devil bound by earthly laws?' he asked with soft menace. 'Get into the car.'

Walk openly into the jaws of hell? Cressy's pointed chin lifted. 'No!' She wanted to turn and march away but her legs were on strike. By keeping her knees locked she managed to stop them trembling.

'You want me to come out there and get you?'

'You just try!' she said fiercely, knowing full well he could do it with very little effort. She doubted if she had the strength to even run.

He knew it, too. He closed his eyes and tilted his head back against the padded seat-rest. Gradually the set expression on his face eased. When he had himself under control he looked at her again, her frazzled face and the outrageous hair caught up in an exploding pony-tail that danced behind her head.

'Do you know how far you've come?'

Cressy shrugged warily, not trusting his calm. 'Quite a way.'

'Two kilometres. In how long?' She remained stubbornly silent and he followed up his advantage. 'Look at you! You look as if you've run a marathon. I bet you're dehydrated already. You're *supposed* to be convalescing——'

'You mean I'm supposed to be safely under guard, well out of the way of your Thugs' Think Tank——'

'What makes you say that?' he said sharply.

'Because they all looked like thugs when I first saw them, you included. Oh, come on, Devlin.' She took a step towards the open door, the better to taunt him. 'You may have shut me in my room but I'm not deaf and dumb, or totally ignorant. You should have painted out my window if you didn't want me to recognise one or two of the famous faces taking their daily constitutional round the gardens. The red setter is Sir Peter Hawthorne, the petrochemical chief, and the roly-poly dachshund is Kurt Matheson, the Coal King. I bet the rest are all captains of industry, too. No wonder you're paranoid about security. Someone could come in and rid the country of its top dogs in one swoop. You needn't have bothered to eavesdrop on my calls, you know. I don't number terrorists among my friends.'

'That remains to be seen,' he muttered, neither confirming nor denying her statement. 'What makes you think I monitored your call?'

'The telephone in your bathroom where you conveniently retreated for a non-shave.' Her knees weren't doing their job so Cressy dared lean against the door, grateful for the extra support. The cool shade of the interior behind the tinted windscreen was an appeal she found it hard to resist.

'What the hell were you doing in my suite?' His look of outrage was as good as a confession.

'Snooping,' she told him, enjoying the upper hand for once. 'It's your fault for being so secretive. Surely you didn't expect me to respect *your* privacy when you didn't respect mine?' She decided to turn the screws a little more. 'Actually, I really just wanted to check whether the mirror above my bed was one-way. I was a bit suspicious when I saw that your bathroom mirror was positioned back to back with the one in my room.'

His fury intensified. 'You thought I put you in there to satisfy some private perversity——!'

He obviously resented aspersions being cast on his sexuality. Cressy filed that titbit away. 'You must admit that keeping me a prisoner in a room decorated like a brothel seems a bit kinky!'

'That room was decorated by my mother——' he bit off savagely.

'Your *mother*!' Cressy's eyes widened as her perception of the Spanish aristocracy took an abrupt nose-dive. 'What was she, a——?' She just managed to control her unwary tongue, warned by the nameless threat which briefly darkened his eyes to the colour of a sultry sky. She coughed and flexed her shoulders uneasily under the pale blue blouse, edging her hip against the temptingly soft passenger seat, taking the weight off her tired limbs. She wanted to know more! 'Er—it's so different from what I've seen of the rest of the house.'

'It was intended to be.' He studied her leaning figure for a moment. 'It's a long story.' He paused, and she leaned some more, her cinnamon eyes spiced with fascinated curiosity. He turned off the guttural engine and moved sideways on the bench seat in an attitude of unthreatening relaxation. He opened the pocket in the dashboard of the pick-up and took out a chocolate bar and unwrapped it. He took a bite, and those huge eyes fastened intriguingly on his mouth. The tip of a pink tongue crept out and touched the corner of rosebud lips. Devlin mirrored the movement and retrieved a sliver of chocolate. 'It was the master bedroom when my parents lived here. Want some?'

Cressy's eyes rounded even more as she took an absent bite out of the snack bar he casually extended. His *parents* had slept amid all that sinful vulgarity?

'No...it wasn't that my father required the extra—er—stimulation?' Devlin murmured, reading her mind, watching her blush bloom into full flower, clashing hideously with the carroty curls that wisped free around her damp temples. He offered her another bite, getting an extraordinary satisfaction when she accepted, as if she were a wild creature he was gentling to his hand.

'My mother was—*is*—a possessive woman and has a very Latin temperament. She didn't like it when my father flirted with other women, even though no one in their right mind would call a rough diamond like Dad a ladies' man. He was irresistible to her and she simply couldn't see that he wasn't irresistible to every other woman. They had an awful row one night when I was about sixteen. My father stormed away on a business trip and when he came back he found that his pleasantly masculine master suite had been transformed into surroundings "more fitted to his character". He was so furious he dragged her in there to show her exactly what his character was. They didn't come out for two days...' He trailed off suggestively and Cressy nearly choked on a lump of chocolate.

She was no prude, but she didn't think that was any way to talk about your parents. She knew that Max had had fleeting relationships with women all over the world since her mother died, but to actually face the reality of your parent . . . well . . .

'And then they moved into the suite next door,' Devlin continued relentlessly, 'where I am now. But they never redecorated that other room. And whenever they had a fight, that's where they made up. It's called the Reconciliation Room. Why don't you get in, Cressy?' he continued smoothly, without a break. 'You know you want to. I promise I won't hurt you. In fact I think I've got another chocolate bar in here somewhere, if you'd like it. Seiver said you didn't eat much of a breakfast.' He searched through the deep pocket and found it, placing it on the seat beside him.

Cressy eyed it hungrily and Devlin felt an irritating pang of guilt, as if he were a dirty old man offering candies to lure an unsuspecting child into his clutches. But he had no guarantee that she was as innocent as she looked, he reminded himself grimly. Just because she had baby-big eyes and a mouth that looked as soft as an unfurled bud and a face sweet enough to warm the devil's soul, it didn't mean a thing. She had shown signs of being as hard as nails under that sweetheart exterior, and her presence here now was proof. Her determination might provoke his admiration, but her fearlessness was chilling and her wilful single-mindedness made her a positive menace, to herself as well as to others. She was in no way unsuspecting, either. She was as mistrustful of him as he was of her. If she dropped her guard now it was entirely her own fault. So why did he have a sudden urge to warn her not to be taken in by his soft words? He swore under his breath. His misplaced protectiveness was a complication he couldn't afford. But, dammit, even if he risked letting her go, in her condition she wouldn't get very far and he'd only

have to pick her up and put her back together all over
again, thus giving her even more reason to resent him.

'Come on, Cressy. Game over. I've wasted enough
time as it is coming after you,' he growled abruptly.

'Why did you, then?' she demanded, wondering if she
could snatch the bar without him snatching her.

'Because you could have got lost out here and died of
exposure. This is a big property, you know. We have
bush, bogs, concealed creeks...any number of places
you could fall and lie for days before you were discovered, if ever. Do you think I want that on my
conscience?'

'I didn't know you had one.'

'If I didn't I wouldn't be here. Believe me, you're a
problem I'd much rather be rid of!'

His harshness was far more convincing than his honey.
Besides, black spots were dancing in front of her eyes.
Cressy hoisted herself up on to the warm vinyl seat and
picked up the chocolate bar in one smooth motion. Not
for the world would she thank him, though.

'I *could* have got away, you know. If I were my usual
self,' she said, opening the wrapper with her teeth.

'I shudder to think what that might be,' he said drily,
watching her devour the bar, aware that she was very
probably right. She wasn't short on intelligence, just
common sense. 'Sorry there isn't any more chocolate,
but it's not very good food value, anyway. You can have
some soup and steamed vegetables when we get back.'

'I'm not hungry any more.' In fact, she felt slightly
sick, trying to rid her mouth of its sweet coating. 'I am
thirsty, though. I'd love an ice-cold Coke.'

'Orange juice is better for you.'

'I happen to like Coke!'

'Do you know what's in it?'

'I don't care what's in it, it tastes good. My God, don't
tell me you're a health junkie!' said Cressy in horror.

'I never carry anything to the point of obsession,' he
said coldly. 'But I do believe in eating sensibly.'

'Then what are you doing driving around with chocolate in your glove compartment for?' demanded Cressy
triumphantly.

'This is the farm vehicle. I rarely use it.' He pricked
her smugness with effortless ease as he started the engine
and turned back for the house.

'But you ate some,' she pointed out doggedly.

'Only to bait the trap. And I succeeded rather well,
wouldn't you say?'

'I only got in because I was tired,' said Cressy, in a
weak attempt to wipe the smug expression off his face.

'Probably years of unhealthy eating catching up with
you. Chester said that you didn't seem to have taken
very good care of yourself.'

'Oh, shut up!'

'Sore loser, Cressy?'

Yes, she was. In fact, Cressy's sense of humour was
not her strongest point. As a child she had been teased
about her hair colour and her temper, and the label of
hot-head still dogged her although she had proved over
and over in her work that she wasn't. There was also her
clumsiness, that was *always* good for a joke, but the
laughs had worn a bit thin over the years. Then there
was her regrettable tendency to fall in love with the wrong
kind of men, ones who were attracted by her sweet looks
or her professional reputation rather than her true personality, and who ended up feeling cheated when the
usual saga began: forgotten dates, crushed flowers,
demolished crockery and an inexplicable reluctance to
go to bed with the same swift, luminous enthusiasm that
she took photos. The trouble was, she had decided, that
she was a slave to her love for animals. If a man reminded her of a cuddly bear or a playful seal, or a silky
squirrel, she just couldn't help herself opening her heart
to him. Usually she was every bit as disappointed as they
were, but she still kept blundering on...hoping...

'If people have to lose they shouldn't be forced to
enjoy it as well,' she grumbled. 'Why should they be

punished twice? I bet you're not such a good loser
yourself.'

'I'm better at winning,' he admitted simply.

Cressy brooded on that. The implication was that he
didn't lose very often. Unfortunately it was all too easy
to believe. There was such an impregnable air of *certainty* about him ...

Cressy was chagrined to discover that the drive back
to the house took only a few minutes. All that effort to
so little effect, she fumed, as Devlin drew to a halt outside
the huge slab of kauri that was the front door. He gave
a light toot on the horn as he did so and the front door
was opened a few moments later by Frank Drake.

'I see you found her,' he said drily.

'Only because I let him,' Cressy said sourly.

'Oh, of course,' he soothed her small sting of humiliation with a smile. Frank liked her, she knew, in spite
of the fact that she was obviously a damnable nuisance.

But Devlin had seen something in Frank's expression
that she hadn't. 'Is anything wrong?'

'It depends on your point of view.' Frank shrugged
and looked at Cressy. 'I think Seiver is holding some
lunch for you in the kitchen.'

She was being dismissed, but politely. She really only
wanted to flop into bed, but one look at Devlin's impatient expression propelled her tiredly into the kitchen
as the two men turned their backs on her for a low-voiced
discussion.

In the kitchen Seiver greeted her with his usual lack
of diplomacy.

'So you're back! I told them you wouldn't get far. No
stamina.'

Just to annoy him she insisted on sitting at the kitchen
table to slowly plough her way through the big bowl of
chunky soup and several thick slices of bread and butter
he had heaped on a tray, taking her time with each
blatantly reluctant mouthful, spinning out her insulting
presence as long as she could. They were glaring at each

other when Devlin entered, frowning, and immediately contributed to the malevolent atmosphere.

'Why didn't you take it upstairs for her, Seiver? She should be back in bed after the workout she's had this morning.'

'She refused to go, and I didn't think you wanted any more rough stuff,' Seiver said, with a sullen air of injured self-righteousness.

'Particularly since you'd probably come off worst, like last time.' Cressy sneered at him.

He sneered back. 'Last time I was under the mistaken impression you was a little lady, not a hulking great she-devil shrew.' His blue eyes cut to Devlin. 'Either she stays out of my kitchen, or I do. An' I don't suppose she's much of a hand at cookin', not the way she turns up her dainty nose at good plain food.'

Devlin looked at Cressy in disbelief. 'Are you just a naturally disruptive force or do you actually make an *effort* to bring trouble into everyone's lives?'

Cressy only had time to steam silently at Seiver's sly grin of triumph before she was hauled out of the room. This time she wasn't hustled upstairs to her velvet-lined prison, but to a small, high-tech office next door to the kitchen. Her jaw dropped when she saw the decorations on the walls: a series of grainy black and white photographic prints depicting miners and oilmen at work and in crisis.

'You're his daughter, aren't you?' Devlin said as he monitored her recognition. 'Max Cross is your father.'

Cressy smiled reminiscently, ignoring the hint of accusation. The series he had shot twenty years ago for Magnum, the French Press photo agency, had won Max a prestigious international award, one of many he had been accorded in his long career. Now in his late fifties he still lived at the same pace he had in his twenties. As long as he could click a shutter he would never retire.

'Are you going to deny it?' Devlin asked harshly.

'What? No, of course not. Why should I? I'm proud of my Dad.' The impact of the prints was the same, however many times she saw them.

'Then why hide it?'

The accusation was now inescapable and it bewildered her as she turned to face him. 'I don't hide it. On the other hand, I don't go around introducing myself as Max Cross's daughter, either. I'm not a cipher, you know, I do have a life and a successful career of my own, which I didn't just inherit from Daddy!' She regretted the pointed dig as soon as it was out, so she tried to be more conciliatory. 'It was because of Dad's reputation that I used my middle name as a professional name when I started out——'

'As a wildlife photographer...'

'Well, I didn't become an expert right away,' she said, nettled by his overt sarcasm. 'In the circumstances it was only natural, I suppose, that I'd start off in news. A lot of photographers do their apprenticeship that way, it gives you a variety of on-the-job training and experience that's hard to beat——'

'But you still occasionally work for newspapers. You are now, for example...'

'Only as it impinges on my field.' Normally Cressy was modest about her talents, but then, she wasn't used to having them so flagrantly undervalued. 'I'm not some hack that has to accept every job that comes along. I'm a damned good photographer in a very esoteric field! These days I can and do pick and choose my jobs. And what I *choose* to do, pretty well exclusively, is work for organisations like the World Wide Fund for Nature, or *National Geographic*. At the moment I have an ongoing commission with the New Zealand Conservation Department, documenting their work with endangered native species...hence the wetas. I'm only doing it for the newspaper because it happens to conveniently fit in with my plans——'

'Where is he now...your father?'

Cressy shrugged, impatient with the change of subject. 'I don't know, he moves around a lot, and so do I. Why, do you want his autograph?'

'He must be a very interesting man,' Devlin surprised her by saying quietly, almost against his will. 'Tough to live up to. How did your mother cope?'

'She died when I was about five. I don't remember much about her. She was a journalist, and as far as I can gather she was as footloose and as eager for adventure as Dad.' Cressy thought it was about time *he* answered some questions. 'Does this have anything to do with what Frank told you? Have you been making more enquiries about me?'

He chose to evade answering in the neatest possible way. 'James rang. Your car's been found—abandoned in Hamilton.'

Cressy's eyes brightened with hope. 'With all my gear?'

He spread the big, blunt hands. 'All gone, except for a few clothes. But the Hamilton police have a good lead. It might only be a matter of time...'

'*No!*' Cressy collapsed on to the nearest object, a leather wing-chair, her hands balled in frustration.

'Surely you must have had it insured——?'

'Yes, but it's not *that*!' The artist in Cressy was outraged to despair. 'It's got nothing to do with money, and everything to do with value. It's taken me *years* to collect exactly what I want, to break it all in exactly to my liking, to get used to the individual quirks of each separate piece. It's not just an assembly of bodies and lenses, it's...that stuff has *soul*! Macro-photography is all about precision, about perfection. It'll take me ages to get used to new gear! Thank God I kept my Olympus with me. Which you haven't yet returned, by the way,' she added grimly. 'And you'd better or I'll make such a fuss you'll realise the disruption I've caused so far is nothing to what I *can* do——'

'Actually I have it right here,' he said smoothly, producing the familiar black case from a filing cabinet drawer. 'Unfortunately the film inside was accidentally exposed, but otherwise it just has a superficial scratch or two.'

Cressy snatched it off him and quickly checked it over. She didn't doubt that the film had been exposed deliberately, but since it had been blank anyway she wasn't going to bother to argue.

'It's a pretty old model for a professional photographer to use, isn't it?' Devlin watched her hands move over the camera almost caressingly.

'It's my good luck camera. My father gave it to me when I was ten.' She pulled a wry face. 'Mind you, he made me use my pocket money to buy my own film. Otherwise, he said, I wouldn't value it. Every shot must tell a story—have a frame of reference and a point. If they don't then they're just meaningless images, only useful as personal mementoes...'

Devlin found that he was suddenly deeply curious about her work. If she was as good as she claimed to be, and Frank had said he had it on excellent authority that she was, then her photographs would probably reveal far more about Cressida than she herself would. A camera could frame a lie, but the lie lay only within the frame. The concept *behind* the image, the artistic vision that had generated and articulated it, would always be a true expression of the artist. He needed to know the truth about Cressida Cross, for his own personal, private reasons as well as the obvious ones...

Cressy looked up, caught the oddly covetous expression on his face and hurried into speech. 'Did I have any extra film with me? I usually carry some...'

His hesitation was so slight that she might have imagined it. 'Yes, you did. It got wet but it may be OK.' He retrieved it from the file. 'Here!'

She caught it on the full. 'These casings are designed to be watertight. Of course if it's been *accidentally* exposed——'

'It hasn't.' He coolly returned her sly look and she knew then that the simple act of tossing her the tiny canister had been more an act of faith than of reason, and part of him was already regretting it.

'How far can I trust you, I wonder?' he murmured without much hope of an answer. He got one anyway.

'Probably as far as I can trust you?'

He shrugged, the scarred side of his face turned away from her as he glanced out of the window, and she was made freshly aware of how beautifully structured were the bones of his skull. His looks must have verged on arrogant perfection before age and experience and his injury made their inroads into youthful splendour and turned it into a tough masculinity that some women might find too aggressive for their taste. No wonder Nina said she thought of sex when she thought of Devlin Connell. And he had heard every word! Had he been flattered or amused? Cressy thought probably amused. She sensed that he wasn't a man who was easily flattered, or cared to be. A pity her camera wasn't loaded. She would like to take a shot of him like that, backlit by the window, brooding, handsome...and then another shot, highlighting the scar, the pale accusing eyes...like Janus, two faces to the one man...and then the composite face revealing the total complexity... Her trigger finger itched.

'Would you let me shoot you?'

'I bet you'd like to,' he said drily, interpreting her literally. 'I thought you concentrated on wildlife these days.'

'You *are* wildlife. A panther, remember... You'd make an interesting study of domestic adaption.'

His eyes narrowed, the predator sizing up a prey. 'I might consider it...providing that you agree not to try and run off like that again, to stay a few more days until

Chester can discharge his medical responsibilities with a
clear conscience. If the police are as on the ball as they
seem to be you might even get your gear back before
you leave...'

Cressy knew that she wasn't in any condition to work
yet...today had proved that beyond doubt. But to stay
here—that would be *courting* the danger that she had
been so anxious to escape...and she wasn't talking about
physical danger!

'I suppose you want me to agree to make it less hassle
for you to keep me prisoner,' she accused warily.

'No imprisonment. You're free to wander, just not
outside the gates without checking with me first, please.'

'*Please?* My, you are going overboard,' Cressy teased,
knowing she was mad to even consider his offer, let alone
tease him about it.

'As a celebration of our truce, why don't you join us
for dinner tonight?' he said softly.

'Us? You mean, you and Frank?'

'And my various other guests...' He paused tantalisingly while she vainly tried to hide her shock at his sudden
concession, and the leap of curiosity inevitably followed. 'I'm sure they'll be just as interested to meet you
as you are to meet them.'

'What's the catch?' asked Cressy, now as deeply suspicious as she was intrigued.

'No catch. All you have to do is behave with reason-
able discretion. As far as anyone else is concerned, you're
my invited guest, an independent young woman who's
had the misfortune to be very ill and now only requires
a little gentle cosseting to fully recover. No more or less
than the truth, after all...'

CHAPTER FOUR

'OH, DEAR! I'm most terribly sorry. Here, let me mop that up for you.' Cressy grabbed her napkin and began dabbing ineffectually at the puddle of wine in the lap of the man on her left.

'It's all right, Miss Cross, really, I can do it myself...' David Eastman squirmed uncomfortably, conscious of the ill-concealed smirks around the dinner table. He caught Cressy's wrist, taking the napkin off her and attending to himself.

'I'm really sorry, David, I just didn't look where I was putting my hand...' He looked rather startled and Cressy suddenly realised what he thought she meant and blushed. 'I was talking about my knocking over your glass of wine,' she added, blushing even further when he laughed.

'Cressida!'

She turned her head reluctantly to her right where Devlin sat at the head of the table. He was glaring at her with an icy intensity, his exclamation having been delivered with equal iciness. 'I think you're getting a little tired——' he began pointedly.

'Nonsense,' Cressy cut him off with a glare of her own, her blush paling rapidly. 'I'm enjoying myself. You're not getting rid of me yet!' she added in a fierce undertone that only he could hear, ignoring the flare of temper in his eyes.

If he didn't want her here it was just too bad. He had made the invitation, and then tried to renege on it when he conveniently remembered that she didn't have anything suitable to wear. To make his point in what he obviously thought was a subtle manner he had ordered an early dinner tray sent up to her room with a note

saying he would get a dress for her the next day, but
Cressy had refused to be placated. He had probably never
really intended to let her dine with them. It had just
been a token gesture to keep her temporarily quiet. But
he had underestimated Cressy yet again. She had often
been in situations where she had to make something out
of nothing. She was a great improviser!

It hadn't taken her long to whip up an ensemble. She
had donned her famous purple slip, laundered at last,
and used the gold brocaded sash of the floor-length cur-
tains from her room as a cummerbund to gather and
hold up the red lace tablecloth that had graced a small
stand in the corner. She had stood on the bed to look
at herself in the big mirror and decided that she didn't
look half bad...a bit blindingly colourful, especially with
her hair waving wildly about her shoulders—Seiver had
enjoyed telling her they didn't have a hair-drier in the
place—but in an attractive, dramatic sort of way. Fortunately the lacy straps of her slip were broad enough
to tuck her bra straps under, because even Cressy knew
the difference between style and indecency!

She had listened at the door of her room until there
were no more sounds from the upper floor, deliberately
delaying her entrance until she thought that they had
had time for a couple of mellowing drinks. She followed
the sound of masculine voices and found the long, cream-
panelled dining-room, furnished only with a huge rect-
angular polished wood table and a dozen matching
chairs. It was the same room she had blundered into that
first night, she recognised vaguely, and the same mob
was in attendance. Eight men in suits, standing around
in bunches of twos and threes, talking over drinks. Devlin
and Frank were half turned away from her in a discussion at the far end of the room. Cressy quickly and
quietly attached herself to the nearest group, introducing herself with a charming apology for being late.
The three men, Sir Peter Hawthorne included, fell over
themselves to reassure her that she was worth waiting

for. Others began to drift across and Cressy was kept busy juggling names and faces, but still she was aware of the exact moment that Devlin spotted her. An instant later he was at her side, a big hand clamped warningly on to her elbow, asking her with lethal pleasantness what she was doing. Quickly she went into her poor, helpless invalid act.

'Oh, Devlin,' she simpered, 'you're such a *darling* to let me upset all your arrangements. I'm afraid I was getting so bored and lonely up there all by myself I was in danger of making myself ill all over again,' she told her attentive audience. Their faces were sympathetic, amused, affable. Only Devlin still looked like a mobster, face carved out of an impressive piece of granite, a muscle flicking in his jaw. '*Dear* Devlin knew I needed taking out of myself and I did so *beg* him to let me come down. I just hope I'm not trespassing too much on everyone's goodwill. And I hope you've all forgiven me for the *awful* exhibition I made of myself that terrible night I arrived...'

The response was gratifying and Cressy tossed Devlin a smug look as she sweetly brushed aside his gritty expressions of insincere concern until he broke out tautly, 'Just make sure you don't tire yourself out. If I see you flagging, it's straight back upstairs!' And she knew that he would use the slightest excuse to carry out his thinly veiled threat.

'Now, Connell, I can see why you wanted to keep this delightful creature all to yourself, but you mustn't be selfish.' Sir Peter took her hand and tucked it through his elbow, a slight shading of malicious amusement in his voice as he misinterpreted his host's reluctance. 'She needs a bit of extra attention to put the roses back in those pale cheeks, and if you can't or won't give it to her, don't begrudge us the welcome opportunity...' And with that he promptly took her under his wing, introducing her to those she hadn't yet met. No one seemed to resent the loss of the 'stag' atmosphere of the past

few days, and Devlin's evident disapproval at her appearance only seemed to egg his guests on in their enthusiasm to make Cressy welcome. She got the distinct
impression that thwarting Devlin was a novelty they all
intended to enjoy to the hilt, and their natural competi-
tiveness added spice to the provocation.

For there was no doubt that out in the real world they
were definitely competitors. Apart from Sir Peter and
Kurt Matheson, Cressy knew two others, if only by
reputation—Sir Edward Davies, head of New Zealand's
largest forestry company, and Hugh Alton whose high-
profile interests included some lucrative gold mines. The
remaining two, Steven Kane and David Eastman, she
discovered in the course of the evening were also involved in primary resource management—gas and oil
exploration and hydroelectric power management re-
spectively. Given the least excuse they would probably
gobble each other's companies up without a qualm, so
what were they all doing playing all-friends-together
down on the farm? Cressy wondered anew. But then,
what did she know about the mysterious workings of the
upper echelons of big business? Maybe they were all
members of a Lodge, or a Rotary Club or a secret society
of millionaires. Maybe Devlin discreetly rented out his
magnificent house to business seminars...

Thankfully, given her unworldliness in business
matters, the dinner conversation was kept light and un-
taxing, as befitted an invalid. Most of the men being on
the wrong side of middle-age, they tended to treat her
with the kind of flattering indulgence they might show
towards a favourite niece. Without the benefit of make-
up Cressy knew she probably looked very young in their
eyes, and Devlin's occasional needling comments seemed
to imply that she was not only young but also helpless.
When Sir Peter had asked if she had a job Devlin was
quick to precede her with an answer.

'Cressy dabbles in photography, don't you, darling?'

Dabbles? Darling? Cressy was incensed at his flippancy. 'Actually I——'

'Actually she's rather good. Making quite a name for yourself, aren't you, Cressy, in your own little way?' Devlin chucked her under the chin as if she were a baby, and not a particularly bright one at that, making 'your own little way' sound slightly indecent. 'Not that she has to try very hard to connect the name Cross with photography in the public mind. She's had all the advantages of a lucky birth to help her. Her father is Max Cross...'

Of course, that was the end of the polite interest in a mere girl's career. They all wanted to know the truth behind some of Max's more dramatic exploits and Cressy ruefully obliged, not really offended. Max's life *was* infinitely more exciting than her own and, charming as her companions might be to talk to, they were from a generation brought up in an atmosphere of ingrained male chauvinism, so she couldn't blame them for their attitude. Devlin, however, she could and did blame. He had deliberately made her sound nothing more than the daffy, dilettante offspring of a famous man.

Normally she would have been a little shy among so many strangers, but Cressy's desire to revenge herself on Devlin made her bold. She discovered that it was very pleasant to be the focus of so much flattering male attention. It went drastically to her head, far more so than the wine that Devlin had flatly refused to serve her would have. And she noticed that the more brilliantly she sparkled, the more darkly Devlin smouldered. And the expression of horror that had flitted across his face when he had finally worked out what it was about her gypsyish outfit that looked so familiar had made her break out in delicious giggles.

Devlin had insisted on seating her at his left hand, but his scheme to hem her in with Frank on her other side was thwarted when David Eastman, who in his midforties was the youngest of the male guests, quickly claimed precedence. His interest and amusing flow of comments was almost enough to enable her to ignore Devlin's brooding surveillance. Almost.

Unfortunately her determination to enjoy herself in spite of him didn't cure her carelessness. David's glass of wine was the second that she had knocked over, the first being Devlin's, though he had been spared damage to his suit, only his pale green silk shirt receiving splatters of the vintage claret. She had also elbowed several pieces of cutlery to the floor and one of the peas from her plate had shot off her fork and skipped down her front during the main course. It had lodged securely in her bra but she hadn't wanted to draw everyone's attention by fishing down her neck. David had proved himself a gentleman by pretending not to notice but Devlin had given her a searing look that told her he believed that her every move was custom-tailored to irritate and embarrass him. The resultant anxious desire not to make another gaffe made her hastily decline the obvious risk inherent in the chasing of delicious melon balls around her dessert plate, but then she had to suffer through the mild torture of being tempted, titbit by titbit, from David's plate. Everyone seemed to find this very entertaining and Cressy found the attention that had earlier enlivened her rapidly palling.

'If everyone's finished, why don't we go through to the lounge for our port and let Seiver clear away in peace?' Devlin said sharply, rising to his feet the instant the dessert plates were emptied, and everyone automatically responded to the arrogance of authority. Unfortunately Cressy, whose ingenuity hadn't extended to shoes, knocked her toe on the table leg as she did so and she staggered, right into Devlin's waiting arms.

'I think you've had as much company as you can take for tonight, haven't you, Cressy?' he hissed, gripping her tightly, pushing her backwards. 'Let me see you upstairs, *darling ...*'

'I'm fine,' she said hurriedly. She had to avoid being alone with Devlin until he had had a chance to cool. Frank had kindly warned her that his boss had a temper to match his nickname, incandescently hot and lightning-swift. People scorched by it sometimes swore that Devlin in a rage left the faintest hint of sulphur lingering in his wake. 'I just stubbed my toe. See?' She showed him.

'You're not wearing shoes!' He seemed even more affronted at the discovery than he had been by the realisation that she was wearing a tablecloth.

'I didn't think that sneakers or my ragged slippers would go with my borrowed finery,' she mocked.

'Dammit, Cressy!' He turned her slightly away from the intrigued glances that were coming their way from the men reluctantly letting Frank usher them out of the room. 'Don't you think you've done enough tonight?'

'What? What have I done?' she demanded softly, her courage bolstered by those same glances. 'I've been perfectly discreet. I haven't asked any awkward questions or talked out of turn——'

'No, you've just flaunted yourself half naked and groped the guests,' he bit off crudely.

'I'm perfectly well covered——'

'I can see right through that flimsy tablecloth——'

'Only if you're looking!'

'You think no one else was? They may be a generation older than you but they're not dead. And that's a damned petticoat—— '

'I've got evening tops that show more——'

'I can see your nipples!' he hissed furiously, and Cressy felt a hot flush sweep over her skin.

'T-that's a pea,' she stuttered furiously, putting her hand down her cleavage and rummaging for the evidence. 'See?' She produced it and threw it at him, making another small mark beside the wine stains.

'Then you must have lost another two down there,' he growled tightly, his eyes on the thrust of her breasts.

'Or has fondling a man old enough to be your father turned you on?'

'I wasn't fondling him,' Cressy spat back, her temper hotting up. 'You just see what you want to see. Don't blame me if your imagination is as dirty as your mouth——' To her horror Cressy discovered that his blatant staring was making a liar of her. The way his experienced eyes stripped her made her very aware of her body beneath its thin covering. She felt an odd tingling in her stomach that swiftly spread up and out over her breasts, creating a sensation not unlike a warm hand splayed across the twin peaks. His mouth curved mockingly and his eyes rose to hers, his eyebrows lifting as he dared her to acknowledge what her body already had.

'Go to hell, you hypocritical devil!' she flung at him furiously.

'Eastman is married, and has twin daughters your age,' he said evenly, her rage seeming to cool his.

'So? We were just talking!'

'Flirting.'

She gaped. 'I was not!'

'Not you. Him.' Her mouth dropped open further. 'In business I'd trust him with my life's savings, privately he's a compulsive womaniser...he flirts as he breathes. So I hope you weren't taking his attentions to heart——'

'I'm not the complete idiot you seem to be trying to make out I am,' Cressy snapped, furious with him for spoiling her pleasure with his insinuations. 'As it happens I only go for younger men. Anyone over thirty-five is over the hill as far as I'm concerned. And forty, well, just the *idea* of going with a man that old is *repulsive!*'

In the mood he was in it was reckless to goad him but it was too late to recall the words. Cressy could practically see his tail lashing with fury as his whole body tautened with outrage at the insult to his masculinity and her nostrils twitched, expecting to scent sulphur. Oh, my, he was touchy about his age!

'Are you going upstairs quietly, or do I have to toss you over my shoulder and carry you there myself?' he said quietly at last, a pantherish smile touching his mouth as he observed her increasing restlessness during the deliberately prolonged silence.

Cressy eyed him nervously for a moment. He was bluffing. He *had* to be. He wouldn't risk a scene. That farce of dinner had proved she was safe on that score.

She turned, tossing her head so that her hair sprayed teasingly against his pearl-buttoned shirt, and sashayed smartly across the hall into the lounge, casting only a brief glance over her shoulder to check that he wasn't roaring after her. He wasn't. He was standing, stockstill where she had left him, watching her with an arrested expression. She smiled in triumph at having successfully called his bluff. He responded instantly to the unconscious challenge, his eyes narrowing and dropping. Now it was her bottom that warmed under his pointedly sexual appraisal and Cressy quickened her step, almost falling over herself in her hurry to get safely out of his line of vision. Over the hill? Who was she kidding. Devlin was over the hill only if Mount Everest was on the other side!

She plumped herself hastily down between the incisively brisk Sir Edward and a polite, but largely monosyllabic Hugh Alton on the plush grey couch, but unfortunately Sir Edward proved more of a gentleman than she had anticipated, insisting on striding off to rustle up a cup of coffee for her from Seiver when she refused an offer of port or liqueur. When Cressy felt a hard thigh slide against hers she didn't need to look to know that Devlin had taken Sir Edward's place. Desperately she tried to engage Hugh Alton in deep conversation, but action rather than words must have been the way he'd created *his* empire. Meanwhile Devlin, carrying on an innocuous discussion at large about the quality of the race-horses raised at the stud, moved his thigh insistently against hers, until the only way she could con-

tinue to haughtily ignore his presence was to cross her
legs. As she did so the lace tablecloth pulled free from
the side of her cummerbund, exposing a large curve of
upper thigh. Without looking, or missing a beat of his
conversation, Devlin bunched the lace in his hand and
pulled it up over the bare flesh, tucking it firmly between her crossed thighs. To her fury he left his hand
resting there, intimately tucked against her, a flagrant
act of possession that didn't escape a man in the room.
Cressy tried to surreptitiously dislodge his fingers but
they were still wound in the lace and she was afraid that
if she pushed his hand away or stood up her whole skirt
would come off!

So she had to sit there, smiling and talking, as if she
didn't realise that she was being publicly branded as the
Devil's woman. And, boy, was the Devil enjoying every
moment of her humiliation! Every now and then his
thumb would flex caressingly against her inner thigh to
remind her just who had the literal upper hand. Cressy
feared her teeth would be ground to a powder by the
time she drained the coffee-cup, which was showing an
alarming tendency to rattle in its saucer.

'Cold, darling?' murmured Devlin, eyes flickering
from her shaking cup to her breasts, reminding her of
their earlier contretemps. 'You mustn't get a chill. Here,
take my jacket.'

To her relief he removed the wretched hand to strip
off his jacket and put it over her soft shoulders. But this
was worse! Now she was enveloped in the male warmth
of him, the heady aroma of his body rising all around
her, mingling with her own. Each time she inhaled she
breathed the combination of male and female scents,
complementary and yet contradictory...compellingly
familiar and yet excitingly strange. And the arm that
had solicitously pulled the jacket around her had become
lodged behind her back, his hand now cupping her waist.

Cressy leaned forward to put her half-empty cup on
the coffee-table in front of her. It missed the edge and

fell to the floor. 'Oh, no!' This time Devlin would feel sure she had done it on purpose, a coward's way out...

The iron hand cupping her waist restrained her instinctive forward movement. 'It's all right, Cressy. Seiver will clean it up. Relax, darling...'

She was flushed, as much by his touch as by the knowledge of what he was thinking. 'It was an accident, I just wasn't looking——'

'I know, I know...' Unbelievably, Devlin was soothing her as Hugh Alton gathered up the fallen crockery and handed it to the sour-faced little man who had appeared like magic. 'Don't worry about it, Cressy. Seiver will get you another as soon as he's mopped this up...'

Seiver's answer was a sniff, but Cressy no longer felt like rubbing anyone's nose in her presence. All of a sudden she was deathly tired. Even if she had refused to admit it to Devlin, coming down to dinner had been a bit too much on top of her morning's trek.

'No, it's all right. Actually I...I think I'll just go up to bed,' murmured Cressy, avoiding the smug gleam she knew must be showing in Devlin's eyes, squirming against his hand.

'Oh, you can't deprive us of your company just yet. Why don't you just lean back and relax? No one expects you to scintillate...'

Cressy couldn't believe what she was hearing. This from the man who a few minutes ago had been trying to hustle her off as fast as he could? She knew he had a temper. Knew he was tough. But she had not thought him capable of real cruelty...until now. Her eyes shot to his and found there a warmth of amusement that terrified her.

'I'll take you up in the few minutes, mmm?' he murmured into her wide-eyed stare as he tucked her more firmly into his side. He bent and kissed her small, bewildered mouth, his tongue flickering briefly into its parted sweetness, watching the hectic colour flare along her cheekbones at the flagrant display of desire. He wanted to kiss her again. More than that, he wanted to know if she tasted just as sweet everywhere else. For that reason he wasn't going to take her upstairs until he was sure that he had the wayward urge well under control. But neither was he willing to let her go alone, or let anyone else have the privilege. The thrust of desire was not new to him, he was a man who had always responded eagerly to the challenge of the unexpected, the unusual, but this raging tenderness was, and the fiercely intense sense of ownership. For a man who had always held his possessions lightly, determined never to let them own *him*, that very intensity raised danger signals which in their turn were flagrant challenges. Hard experience had taught Devlin that the most difficult and dangerous mines were usually the ones that offered the richest plunder to those prepared to take the risks. The emotional returns were almost as satisfying as the material rewards when one was recklessly gambling on gut instinct.

Thus he waited until his tension eased and he felt Cressida leaning heavily into him before he drew her to her feet and gently prompted her to make her weary goodnights. Then he picked her up, precisely as promised, and carried her upstairs.

'You don't have to do this,' she said weakly, still blushing at some of the comments that had drifted from behind them when Devlin had paused in the hall to adjust her weight against his chest. She should be furious with him for giving them reason for comment. She should hate being carried around like a feeble weakling...

'Oh, yes, I do. It's my fault you're in this condition. I should have kept you out of mischief by locking your door.'

'It wouldn't have made any difference. I went out the window this morning,' she told him meekly.

He froze, one foot on the stairs. 'You climbed down the *wall*?'

'Oh, no,' she reassured him airily. 'I just swung across the drainpipe to the fire escape. That's what it's there for, isn't it . . . for people to escape?'

'I'll have that damned window nailed shut!'

'You can't. Fire regulations,' she pointed out with a tired smile. 'Can we go up now, or are you just going to stand here and glare at me?'

He was stiffly silent until they reached her room. He set her gently down on the plush red carpet and stepped back, thrusting his hands in his pockets. The movement pulled the shirt tight across his chest.

'I . . . I'm sorry about that stain,' Cressy said tentatively, swaying slightly at the loss of his warmth and strength.

'Also my fault, I guess. I suppose I make you nervous——'

'Oh, no. I'm like that——' She stopped, hand across her mouth, aghast at what she had been going to let slip.

'Like that—what?' he asked, made more curious by her guilty dismay.

'When—er—when . . . I'm tired!' she mumbled, quickly following the lie with a cracking yawn.

He just looked at her thoughtfully, those pale silver eyes revealing nothing. 'What happened to the vase?' he asked suddenly.

'W-what vase?'

'The red and gold Chinese vase that used to sit on the occasional table over there.' Neither of them looked in the direction he indicated.

'Oh, that? Was it valuable?' she asked warily, wondering if Seiver had found the carefully wrapped pieces in the waste paper bin in the bathroom and ratted.

His eyes flickered as he pounced. *'Was?'*

Cressy tried another yawn but it wouldn't wash. Devlin's hands came out of his pockets to rest on his hips. With his head tilted back, his eyebrows raised and that haughty look of enquiry in his eyes he suddenly acquired the mantle of his foreign heritage, looking very much an arrogant Spanish aristocrat confronted with a recalcitrant peon.

'I...I must have brushed against the table...it isn't very solid, you know,' Cressy attempted to deflect his contempt.

'You broke it?'

'I was going to tell you,' she said defensively. 'I'll pay for it, of course.' A chilling thought suddenly occurred to her. Hadn't he said Chinese? 'It wasn't Ming, was it?'

His mouth twitched at her anxiety. 'No, actually. My mother picked it up in a cheap department store. The room was supposed to be cheap and nasty, remember?'

Cressy sighed her relief, her hand fiddling with the curtain sash around her waist. 'Just let me know how much and I'll give you a cheque.'

'If the car thief hasn't cleaned out your bank account,' he pointed out drily.

'I've already informed my bank of the theft,' Cressy informed him tartly. 'They've put a stop on my cheque account and credit card. You seem to have this strange idea that I'm incapable of looking after myself. I don't know how you got that impression——' his eyebrows lifted higher and her chin tilted to match '—but it's quite wrong.'

'Don't forget to add the two jugs, and the plate you dropped in the sink...'

'What?'

'To the total damages bill. Fortunately Seiver isn't going to sue for damages over his split lip and my laundry is taken care of, but you seem to have put your toe through the hem of that tablecloth.'

Cressy looked down. She had. She battled with welling frustration, scowling at him.

'No wonder that camera of yours looks so battered. You're a bit accident-prone, aren't you, Cressy?' he said, with stinging softness.

'No.' Her cornered expression defied him to challenge her, but the leaden tiredness that dragged at her limbs was even more obvious than the lie. She wasn't quite sure how it happened but in the confusion of the next few minutes her skirt and sash were whisked away, her face mopped with a refreshing flannel and softly fluffed dry, and she was flat on her back in bed, Devlin sitting by her hip, one arm braced across her.

'Better?'

He filled her vision, the fingers of his free hand lightly combing through the thick ginger waves that spread across the pillow. The gentle tug on her scalp was very soothing.

'*Si, señor,*' she teased his arrogant efficiency sleepily.

He said something in Spanish and her heavy lids jerked open and she blushed wildly.

'So it's not just phrase-book Spanish you have,' he murmured, caught out in an impulsive indiscretion.

'I understand more than I speak. I've spent quite a bit of time in South America,' she told him huskily, her eyes sliding helplessly down the body that he had just erotically informed her could teach her to say '*si*' in far more satisfying ways.

'And you're used to hearing the words I just used? Did you have a Spanish lover?' he asked, weaving his fingers deeper into her hair, allowing her only a fraction of movement as she tried to shake her head.

'I...I really only got the gist...' she stammered, far more dismayed that he was at the betrayal of his private thoughts.

'You're as red as the sheets,' he said, lowering his head slowly, holding her captive with his eyes as he asked roughly, 'If I said it in English would you burst into flames for me...?'

'Devlin...' She should stop him, she should *want* to stop him! She should push him away, not spread her hands caressingly against his shirt front... What was the matter with her?

'This room is perfect for you. A room of clashing colour and outrageous passion,' he whispered, a breath away from her mouth. 'I can see the questions in your big baby eyes. Very adult questions. You want to know, too, don't you...? You want to know what it would feel like if I——' He lapsed into Spanish again, fierce, flowing and lyrical, wrapping like satin barbed-wire around her mind and body and soul, simultaneously caressing and pricking her to life. She could feel his heart beneath her hands, bucking and plunging like a wild thing against the solid prison of his chest.

'*Devil!*'

'That's what they call me,' he said, swallowing her sigh. He bit her mouth open with raw tenderness. It was even sweeter inside than he remembered, and sinfully evocative of a deeper intimacy. He thrust into her, sheathing his tongue again and again in the hot wet silk, taking shameless advantage of her submission, all his former fine resolve overridden by far more primitive instincts—that of the hunter astride his weaker prey, the miner greedily staking his claim, the male animal exploring his territorial limits. Her small hands slid around his waist, clinging, tightening so that she could pull her body up and into his, fitting herself to his desire. He groaned and relaxed his rigid arms, pressing her down into the firm bed, moving his hips in small, rough, circular rotations to insinuate himself deeper and deeper between her widening thighs. Even through the sheet and feather padding of the eiderdown he could feel her heat welcoming him. He pushed harder. She shuddered beneath him and moaned voluptuously into his mouth and a bolt of pure lightning shot from his groin to his brain, briefly illuminating his insanity. He wrenched his mouth away, rearing back as he dragged in a ragged breath, every muscle knotted against the denial of his craving. To his shock he found himself staring straight into his own eyes.

The mirror above the bed threw back an image of himself that he hardly recognised. He was no innocent. There had been a few occasions when he had made frank use of available mirrors during the act of love, but it had always been just that, a conscious performance, planned and appreciated as such by both participants. This unexpected confrontation was a total shock. He looked like a savage in the grip of some barbaric frenzy, his eyes slitted with lust, his mouth swollen, almost brutal with passion, his big hands staking out the small, trembling woman beneath him like a sacrifice to some nameless, pagan god. It wasn't the first time that Devlin had been forced to acknowledge the dark side of his earthy nature, he knew full well his nickname wasn't entirely unearned, but he had never before seen himself so near to being utterly seduced by it. To his shocked eyes he looked like a man stripped of everything but his sex, a man more than capable of rape in the blind pursuit of mindless, selfish, sensual pleasure... The image burned like acid into his brain. God, he must be terrifying her...!

In spite of her excruciating tiredness it took Cressy a long time to get to sleep after Devlin had left. She couldn't work out what she had done wrong. One moment she had been cresting a glorious, foamy, fizzing wave of passion, the next she had been sharply chastised like a naughty child and practically mummified in the sheets. Devlin had tucked her in so tightly that her sensitised breasts had hurt, but when she had tried to ease the sheet across them he had snapped at her with a ferocity that had brought tears to her weary eyes. It wasn't her fault that he found her lacking as a lover. She didn't have as much experience as he obviously did. Anyway, didn't they say that there were no frigid women, only inept men? It was entirely his fault if he hadn't experienced the wild, exhilarating thrills that she had from the moment his mouth touched hers!

Cressy turned determinedly on to her stomach, squashing away the wretchedly empty ache that Devlin had left her with. He was the one who had started whispering sweet nothings and trying to eat her up! Then, after only the briefest of tastes, he had bolted upright and spat her out as if she were something rotten!

No, not *her* fault at all. It was Devlin Connell who obviously had the problem. She only wished she knew what it was!

CHAPTER FIVE

LYING in the long, sweet grass, Cressy stared up at the wheeling flight of a hawk, envying its strength and freedom. She brought up her camera and followed the bird with the lens until it suddenly swooped and dived down behind some trees. She didn't bother with a shot. Without her two-hundred-millimetre zoom lens there was little point.

She rolled over in the grass, putting her camera down beside her, refocusing her attention on the horses grazing a few metres away. She'd never paid much attention to horse-racing, but after just two days wandering around Rush House Stud she was beginning to realise the fascination that it had for many people. Certainly at close quarters the thoroughbreds were beautiful animals, even though Cressy felt that horses, as with dogs, were not always better off, for all the man-made 'improvements' to breeds.

She got to her feet, moving slowly so as not to startle the mares, two of whom were heavily in foal. As she approached the fence of the small paddock adjoining the stables, Devlin's stud manager, John Hewson, met her.

'Got the pictures you wanted, Miss Cross?'

'Yes, thanks.' Cressy climbed the whitewashed post fence. 'Do you think either of them will foal in the next couple of days?'

'Possible. Rain Lady is pretty near.' John made Hugh Alton seem loquacious, although Cressy had noticed he had plenty to say to his horses.

'Do you think that I might be able to watch, take some photographs?' It was second nature to see the photographic potential in any given situation. She was here, she might as well take advantage of any opportunity that presented itself.

John looked doubtful. 'I don't know. It's a pretty confined space in the stall. You'd need to use a flash, wouldn't you?'

'Not necessarily. It depends on what the available light was like. I might get around it just by using a faster film.'

'I guess we could see what the vet said. And Devlin, of course...'

'I'll be sure and ask his lordship nicely,' she said, with a sweet sarcasm that passed John by.

'Ask me what?'

Cressy spun around, her sneakers slipping in the soft earth on the well-trodden path in front of the stable. Devlin put out a hand to catch her and she batted it away impatiently.

'I thought you were going to fall,' he said mildly. In a thin cream sweater and dark trousers he looked the epitome of a country gentleman.

'Well, I wasn't!' she snapped, detecting a patronising amusement in his innocent remark. 'What are you doing here anyway?' she demanded.

'This is my home, where else should I be?' he said drily.

'I mean out here. Shouldn't you be at a meeting? Don't you have enough people checking up on my whereabouts? Frank, Briscoe, that sneaking Seiver. I can't even take a stroll around the garden without falling over someone with a walkie-talkie. What do you think I'm going to do, steal one of your precious horses and ride off to the nearest fax machine? My *word* isn't good enough for you——'

John Hewson coughed, muttered something about work and sidled, crab-like, on his way.

Devlin regarded her defensive aggression thoughtfully. 'Bored, Cressy?'

'Frustrated would be more like it.' His eyes glinted wickedly and she glared at him. 'I mean *professionally*; because I still haven't got my gear back. I could have used it here.'

'I know a good way to work off that frustration, Red. How about a good hard ride?'

'*What?*' She jolted to a shocked halt. It wasn't difficult to guess which way her thoughts were running. Devlin was flattered, and amused, both of which emotions he wisely concealed behind a bland expression.

'On a horse, Cressy,' he clarified gravely. 'You do ride, don't you?'

Her blush mounted as her wayward thoughts invested his words with an erotic ambiguity. 'Mules,' she said grimly.

'I beg your pardon?' It was either be rigidly polite or betray his wicked amusement by telling her that in that case he was the perfect mount for her—his stubborn tenacity had more than once led to his being compared to that particular animal. But then he would lose her. Already he had deduced that Cressy didn't like being laughed at.

'I've only ridden pack-horses a few times. I usually get mules. Or camels,' she added, wanting to impress on him the breadth of her experience. 'Or elephants. Or——'

He held up his hand. 'I get the picture. You don't want to ride with me. The others are taking a break and I felt like a bit of fresh air before lunch.'

He walked off, back towards the stables, without waiting for her answer. Cressy trudged after him.

'All right, I'll ride, but don't blame me if anything happens...'

She wasn't allowed to ride in her sneakers. In the tack-room she exchanged them and her camera for boots, which had to be stuffed with straw to fit her small feet. Malita was as gentle as Devlin had promised, and as they walked across the yard Cressy's natural confidence reasserted itself. Without making it obvious Devlin put her discreetly through her paces until he was satisfied that she knew what she was doing, then he casually led the way through the back paddock to a stretch of open countryside which led down to a small section of bush intersected by a winding stream. When he gave his own horse her head, the big mare took off in huge bunching strides that Cressy didn't even attempt to keep up with. Devlin was a magnificent rider, she acknowledged ruefully as she watched man and horse flow together in beautiful symmetry. The mare was called Tussore: her hide had the smooth sheen of oiled brown silk, the heavy muscles rippling with each stride, the slender legs seeming almost too fragile to support all that driving power. Such contradictions bred winners and, by John Hewson's account, enough of them to make the Rush House Stud's name synonymous with success.

Cressy didn't fall off and she didn't make a total fool of herself, although she lost her stirrups once or twice. But, lying once again in the soft, thick grass beside the silver stream, she knew exactly who to blame for the feelings sweeping over her!

'Shouldn't we be getting back?'

Devlin rolled on his side. 'Am I boring you?' he teased.

He had been talking about some of his mining experiences, chilling her with the mention of triumph and disaster in equally casual tones, telling her that he always made it a point to spend part of every month at the stud. He had inherited Rush House when his father had retired to his wife's family home in Seville, but the stud had been Devlin's own development. Devlin wasn't a man who enjoyed idleness. He had needed something to come home to and, in the absence of a family, he had met that need by creating a different kind of challenge for himself. When he came home it wasn't so much to rest but to revitalise himself with the change. And everyone expected him to retire next year, retire to his stud and settle for a single challenge for the rest of what would probably be a long and healthy life! Cressy doubted it would satisfy him. Even lying here in the warm noonday sun, he was alive with fascinating thoughts and ideas.

His mocking expression told her that no one, let alone any woman, had ever accused him of being boring. Who was she to disagree? She smothered a polite yawn. 'No, of course not,' she murmured obediently.

There was a small, stinging silence.

'You are a contrary little witch, aren't you?' he said finally, as reluctant amusement overrode his momentary pique. She was deliberately winding him up. But he was no clockwork toy, as she would soon discover!

She raised her eyebrows scornfully. 'I suppose you're used to women hanging on your every word?'

'Why should you think that?' he asked smoothly.

'Because you're——' She stopped, flushing.

It was his turn to raise thick, dark eyebrows. 'What? Handsome? Fascinating? Sexy?'

All that and more! 'You don't think much of yourself, do you?' she said cuttingly.

'I wouldn't have been able to survive in my profession, or in the business world, if I wasn't sure of myself. It's human instinct to attack the weak. I've learned the hard way not to put my trust in people until I know them inside out.'

Cressy sat up, trying to ignore the lazy sprawl of the lean, hard body beside her, and the shattering desire his words aroused. To have Devlin inside her mind...her body... She raised her face to the sun, hoping he would put her flush down to the heat.

'How did you get those scars on your hip?'

She automatically looked down, half expecting them to be showing, but her blouse was well tucked into her jeans.

'I couldn't help but notice them when you were ill,' he said. An explicit picture of him studying her body, touching her with his big hands, popped into her mind.

'A big cat,' she said hurriedly.

'A large tabby?' he teased unthinkingly.

'A panther,' she said succinctly, wiping the smile off his face. 'I inadvertently stumbled across its cub and paid the price for being in the wrong place at the wrong time. I had nightmares for a long time afterwards,' she admitted. 'Did you—about the cave-in?'

So she remembered her clumsy curiosity about his scar. The thought banished his chill of belated fear. 'Yes. And claustrophobia. A rather big handicap for a mining engineer,' he said wryly. 'But I got over it. I enjoyed the job too much to sacrifice it to fear.'

'Besides, the risk is part of the attraction,' Cressy told him knowingly. 'Perhaps even the main part, for you...'

'No, not the main. I will admit it gives life a delicious edge. You must find that, too. I thought your father had the dangerous job, but yours is just as risky, in the sense that you're venturing into the unknown.'

Cressy shook her head emphatically. 'Oh, no, I'm not like Dad, hooked on danger. I couldn't stand that kind of constant tension. What I do is relatively safe. Dad's the risk-taker, the one with all the courage. I'm the quiet, rational, down-to-earth one. That's why I feel so comfortable with nature.'

'You really believe that, don't you?' he marvelled, wondering why she felt the need to flatly reject an integral part of her nature, and shaken by the urge to teach her otherwise. 'You actually see yourself as a pragmatist, more sense than sensibility. You think that, of you and your father, you have the soft option.'

She looked at him uncertainly. 'Well, I do. I'm totally unlike Max. He's a restless spirit, always dashing from crisis to crisis, passionately committed to truth and justice. In fact he's passionate in everything he does. He's nearly sixty and still lives the life of a young man— he's proud of his iron nerves. He just laughs when the bullets start flying. He has a great sense of humour, but you just try and argue with him when he's in one of his stubborn moods! When he makes up his mind about something he's deaf to reason. Sometimes he's incredibly cynical and brutal about his work and at other times he's like an innocent child blundering about at will, completely unconscious of the danger he's in!' Her exasperation was as clear as it was loving.

'And you say you're nothing like him!'

'If you knew Max you'd know it was true.'

He ignored that, tilting his head so that the thick black swathe of hair on his temple slipped to one side. She would have liked to reach out and stroke it back into place, but she didn't know if she would be able to stop there. 'You know, you've just given me a very good description of yourself: stubborn, passionate, blundering about where angels fear to tread, restless, energetic, impatient——'

It was a disturbing picture of herself, not at all the one that she had built her life around. She attacked the greatest slur with gusto. 'I am not impatient! You should see me at work, then you wouldn't call me impatient——'

'Is that an invitation?'

'Yes! You can watch me work on you.' His eyes darkened with an unmistakable message and she explained sternly, 'When I photograph you. You said I could,' she reminded him.

'I said I'd consider it. I don't like having my photo taken, legacy of years being hounded by the Press.'

'Tough,' Cressy said unsympathetically.

'Yes, you are, aren't you?'

He made her sound like an old boot. She lifted her chin. 'Where my work is concerned, yes. When will you pose for me?'

'When you get some replacement gear, I suppose.'

As an evasion it didn't even come close to succeeding. 'I don't need anything but the bare essentials. Artists aren't slaves to their tools the way miners are, you know. I could take a good picture with a cardboard box and a square of light-sensitive paper, if I chose. How about this afternoon?'

'Persistent little devil, aren't you?'

'Takes one to know one. Will you make time for me or not?'

'Oh, yes, I'll make time for you, I can promise you that,' he said with a grim certainty that made her swallow her satisfaction. 'You know, there is one way that you're not at all like your father.'

'What's that?' she said warily, sure she wasn't going to like the answer.

'Your sense of humour. I don't think you have one, or if you do it's buried so deep its probably not worth excavating.'

'I get along fine as I am, thank you very much,' she snapped.

'Mmm, there is a sort of exhilarating sense of challenge about a woman who would rather bite and bark than lick your hand.'

'Lick your boots, you mean. Just because I'm not a yes-woman it doesn't mean I'm a bitch,' said Cressy sourly, helpless to resist his baiting.

'Oh, I hope you won't always say no,' he said silkily. 'And you're not a bitch, Cressy. Since you respond so well to animal analogies I'd say you were...mmm...let me think...' He swept his eyes over her, taking his time, enjoying the rapid turn in the tables.

Certain he was going to say 'armadillo' or 'porcupine', or something equally unflattering, Cressy was taken aback when he said, 'An ocelot, perhaps... Yes, definitely an ocelot...'

Cressy had only seen the beautiful cat once in the wild, in Brazil. The 'tigrillo', as it was called locally, was a solitary forest animal whose disproportionately large eyes were adapted for seeing in the dark. It was about twice the size of a domestic cat, with markings not unlike the jaguar.

'Small but fierce,' Devlin murmured, revealing his unexpected knowledge of the elusive animal. 'It hunts like a shadow, springing from nowhere and bringing its victims down before they even know they're being stalked. But did you know, Cressy, that unlike almost all the other wild cats you can tame an ocelot? If you take it young enough it can become gentle and affectionate enough to play with children...'

Cressy's own eyes were also disproportionately wide. The heat beat down on her head, turning her hair the colour of chilli peppers. 'I...I don't believe in taking animals from the wild,' she said huskily. 'You shouldn't interfere with the natural order of things...'

'Even if it means the death of a beautiful animal who can't ask for the help it needs?' he asked softly, leaning towards her.

'I...even then.' It was a bitter lesson that anyone who worked for any length of time with wildlife eventually learned. You couldn't save every animal from its destiny, and who was to say who had the more right to live, predator or prey?

'Like the ocelot. So beautiful, so fearless, so cruel...' Cressy jumped slightly as he touched her mouth with his finger, tracing the tiny quivering bow, unravelling its control.

She shivered. 'I'm not beautiful...'

'Ah, Cressy, you have so much to learn. Haven't you ever taken a photograph of yourself?'

'No, but Max has—lots of times,' she whispered, hardly knowing what she was saying as he traced the bow again, leaning nearer to study the ripple effect of his touch.

'But he frames you with a father's eyes. I see you as you are, Cressy. If you could see yourself through my eyes you'd know that this was inevitable...' His hands cupped her throat and then slid to smooth her collar, his mouth drifting ever nearer.

'Oh, no, we can't do this, Devlin——'

'Why not?' He flicked open the top button of her blouse, revealing a small triangle of creamy, flushed skin.

'Because, it's not wise...'

'And do you always do the wise thing, Cressida? Was it wise to come riding with me when you knew what I wanted...?' A second button, and the triangle was enlarged.

'I didn't!'

'Liar. You're as curious as I am...' He bent and tasted her pale skin.

'About what?' Helplessly she tilted her head back, making it easier for him.

'About whether the other night was a fluke. I wasn't teasing you, Cressy. If anything it was myself I was torturing...'

She stopped trying to prevent his explorations, her hands tightening in his thick dark hair. 'W-what are you talking about?'

'I didn't want to leave you, Cressy. I would have enjoyed nothing more than spending the rest of the night in your bed.'

'Then why did you stop?' The memory of his rejection still stung.

'It would have been taking advantage.' He was nuzzling inside the crisp cotton now, deeper and deeper towards the scented cleavage, his hands slowly tightening on her hips, turning her upper body towards his. 'You were too tired to think... still not well. I was going too fast for both of us—I didn't want to hurt you... but now you're stronger I think you're ready for this...'

His mouth lifted to hers, as lazily sensuous as his hands and supremely unhurried. He kissed her slowly, lavishly, so intent on his enjoyment that he didn't notice that she had stiffened. In the heat of the moment his words struck her as appallingly cold-blooded. Ready for what? During the very first of her disastrous romances Cressy had blindly succumbed to the heady lure of physical attraction. It hadn't lasted and the disillusionment had been shattering to one who believed firmly in the existence of perfect and passionate love with a single mate. Since then she had forced herself to be more cautious in her relationships and time and time again her caution had proved disappointingly apposite. It had begun to appear that a sudden, sweepingly intense physical attraction to a man was, in Cressy's unfortunate case, a warning not to go within a million miles of him. That made Devlin a million miles too close! Bitterly regretting what she had to do, Cressy clenched her fingers deeper into his hair and yanked his head up, hard!

He gave a yell of pain. 'What the——? What are you doing?'

Cressy whipped up her anger. Of course he was surprised to find out she wasn't utterly overwhelmed by his skilful lovemaking. He thought she was a pushover. He thought she would be flattered by his male desire, happy to be manipulated by it, as women so often were. 'You patronising swine! You obviously think it should always be the *man* who makes the decisions about sex, about where and when and how. The woman doesn't even need to be consulted about the matter. After all, what is a woman but an empty vessel waiting to be filled at a man's leisure? Well, *this* woman likes to make her own decisions... about everything!'

His anger was as quick and purposeful as her own as he grabbed her shoulders, preventing her from rising. 'Really? Is that what you were trying to tell me with those little moans just now? I could have sworn you were urging me on with your "Oh, yes, Devil, yes, please...!"'

Cressy went scarlet at his taunting mimicry. She hadn't known that she had verbalised the dizzying longings he had so swiftly aroused. And to think she had actually *begged*! She had handed him the perfect weapon with which to batter her bruised pride. Well, she had weapons, too!

With a quick, brutal movement Cressy brought her legs up between them and Devlin automatically jerked defensively backwards, losing his grip on her arms. Cressy jumped to her feet, strode to the horses which were blissfully grazing on the lush grass that edged the shade of the small chunk of bush where they had stopped, and gathered up the reins. With an ease that startled human and animal alike, she mounted the little mare and grabbed Tussore's reins as she turned for home.

His aching body and stunned mind a fraction slow on the uptake, Devlin left his lunge too late. He chased her for a few metres, but Cressy had lost her diffidence and chivvied the two horses directly into a gallop. Her laughter swept back to taunt the curses that were turning the air around him blue.

'Who's got no sense of humour now? Better start walking, Your High-and-Mightiness, it's a long way home and it looks like rain!'

CHAPTER SIX

CRESSY didn't pull up the horses until she was well out of sight, and then she had a bit of trouble with the powerfully restive Tussore. She had to calm the horse down before she tackled her flapping blouse, rebuttoning it with shaking fingers. Her breasts were hurting, but not from Devlin's mishandling. His caresses had been slow, languid, the gentle seduction of a man confident of his welcome. The violence had been all hers. It had taken a painful effort to wrench free from the joy of her desiring. If she had let him touch her breasts she would have been completely lost. She knew that because she had wanted it so badly. Too badly. What did she know about him, really? Next to nothing. For all he had talked on the riverbank, he had told her little about the things that really mattered. He had given her plenty of facts about selected parts of his life, certainly, but Cressy knew all too well that facts taken out of their emotional context could be as deceptive as outright lies. She was tired of being deceived by her own misguided feminine instincts.

On the other hand, some instincts were undeniably sound. Like the instinct to escape back to the house. It wasn't only her prediction about rain proving correct that drove her, but also the knowledge that she couldn't go back, even to apologise. Devlin would be as mad as fire. He would want answers, and as yet she didn't have any to give him, none that would make sense, anyhow. Her pride refused to admit that she was running scared.

As she rode on, a light veil of spring rain swept across the countryside, chilling her with mingled apprehension and guilt. Devlin had needed taking down a peg or two, she announced out loud with as much conviction as she could muster. He had been so damned smug about her

inability to laugh at herself; wait and see how amused
he was when the joke was on *him*. She wondered nervously how he would explain his non-arrival if he didn't
get back to the house in time for the rest of his mysterious meeting. Then she stiffened her spine. The damage was done now. She would worry about facing the
music later. At least she didn't have to worry about
Devlin getting lost or falling into the swamps he had
warned her about. He had told her that in spite of his
many absences he knew every inch of his own land. Now
was his chance to prove his boast!

If anyone was going to get lost it would have been
Cressy, but luckily the horses seemed to know their way
and she let them have their heads. Fifteen minutes later,
Cressy was pinning on an airy smile and lying to the
young man who took the horses from her, telling him
that Devlin had asked her to deliver them back to the
stables because they had dallied longer than he had
expected. Well, it wasn't *entirely* a lie, she told herself,
as she ate a hearty lunch under Seiver's hostile eye and
innocently informed Frank that she hadn't seen Devlin
since their ride.

From her room she had a good view of the stables
and back paddocks ... and the steady rain. She was *not*
sitting by the window with an uninspiring novel because
she was worried about him, but because she needed to
be forearmed against his arrival, she told herself. When
he finally trudged into view, at least half an hour after
she had abandoned him, she shuddered in empathy. His
shoulders were bunched under the drenched wool of his
sweater as he climbed the last fence, and rivulets ran
from his plastered hair over the jutting angles of his face
and down his neck. His boots were no longer gleaming
and his jodhpurs were heavily spattered with mud. It
had obviously not been a relaxing stroll!

Cressy half expected him to come crashing in to con-
front her, and when he didn't her relief was tinged with
disappointment, her guilt unresolved. Deciding that she

didn't want him to think she was lurking up there because she was afraid of a confrontation, she went down to the library and mooched around the shelves, looking for something to replace the lacklustre novel, knowing full well that nothing would be absorbing enough to divert her thoughts from the real-life excitement that clashing with Devlin provided.

Instead she unearthed some photograph albums from one of the bottom shelves. All seemed devoted to shots of Devlin and a changing parade of friends, working and carousing with equal enthusiasm. Only Frank seemed a constant face. Cressy appreciated the content, if not the quality of the photos. Perhaps she could satisfy some of her curiosity about Devlin vicariously, by viewing the silent progression from the lithe, tanned boy, in the dustiest book, *sans* scar, surfboard confidently tucked under one arm, tall curvaceous blonde under the other, to the mature man of today. One thing that didn't change about him, she noted sourly, was his taste in women. They were invariably as tall as, if not taller than himself, long-legged and lean-hipped, athletic-looking women who seemed to laugh a lot. Female athletes, she decided maliciously. No wonder he found Cressy difficult to deal with. She didn't fit neatly into the mould. Nor would she want to!

She took the stack of albums over to the couch and shuffled them roughly into what she thought was the proper chronological order, going on the first photo in each. She wasn't aware of the passage of time as she pored over the pages, gaining an appreciation of just how rich and varied Devlin's life had been. Of course, being from a wealthy family had given him a freedom that most young men didn't have, but the photographic evidence showed that his dedication to his job was every bit as intense as his dedication to pleasure. A lot of the pictures were taken in tropical climates—in the East, Papua New Guinea, North Africa and South America—all obligingly labelled in a thick, slashing hand as bold as the man himself. Devlin had worked, ski'd—on water and snow—sailed, climbed, car-raced, cycled, run, swum, glided and partied around the world. There were a number of shots from triathlons and it didn't surprise Cressy to discover that somehow, in his busy life, he found the time regularly to tackle that most gruelling of events, the endurance race in surf carnivals called the Iron-man. Cressy lived a physical kind of life herself, of necessity, but she didn't revel in it the way he obviously did. Now she knew why the meals Seiver served were so relentlessly nutritious. Devlin was as much an athlete as his clutch of bimbos. There didn't seem to be any sport he hadn't attended, as competitor or spectator. Cressy picked up another album and turned the first page. Why, he had even...

When Devlin strode into the library a quarter of an hour later, Frank at his heels, impatient to get through their usually leisured analysis of the meeting's progress, Cressy was still sitting there, holding the album, photographs strewn in her lap and around her feet.

Devlin stopped abruptly, the tension in the room palpable. 'Let's skip it this evening, Frank. Just make a few notes and we'll compare them later...or in the morning.'

'Sure.' Frank grinned. Devlin had been tight-lipped about his belated arrival at the afternoon session; a grim remark about 'trouble with a couple of horses' had been sufficient to excuse him, for everyone knew how valuable his stock was. But Seiver had been more obliging, actually producing a truncated grin himself when he had described Devlin's mud-spattered return from a 'gentle' ride with their resident invalid. The afternoon meeting had been marked by Devlin's sudden impatience with his role of adjudicator. He had abandoned subtlety in favour of a frank, gritty contempt that had achieved more in a couple of hours than they had in the entire previous few days. Talk wasn't cheap, he had said bluntly; it was more expensive than any of them could afford if it wasn't closely followed up with action. They could pass the buck on to someone else, or they could do the job themselves.

'See you at dinner, Cressida.' Frank couldn't help adding, to needle the man in front of him, 'Hope you enjoyed your ride more than the boss did.'

Cressy looked up from the picture she was holding and the pain in her darkened eyes stopped Frank cold. 'What——?'

'Beat it, Frank.'

Frank knew the tone of voice and he didn't argue with it. Neither was he offended by the insultingly brief dismissal. Once or twice in their long friendship he and Devlin had come to blows, but it had never altered their liking or respect for each other. It was because of that bond of respect that they felt free to argue with or insult each other with total honesty. Devlin didn't give his trust lightly, but once given it was absolute.

As the door closed quietly behind Frank, Devlin was already in motion, stalking towards the couch. 'So...not only are you a horse-thief, but you steal my privacy, too.'

The clipped sarcasm hardly touched her; Cressy was still busy assimilating the shock, her face averted. Devlin's voice roughened, sarcasm sliding into revived anger.

'Dammit! You could have sent my horse back, she would have found me. Or perhaps you thought it would be just revenge if a good soaking gave me pneumonia!' Still no reaction. His hands flexed with the desire to shake one out of her. His wounded pride demanded the satisfaction of a response, any response. He refused to be ignored! He leaned over the couch to remove the album from her still hands. 'If you want to know anything about me, Cressy, all you have to do is ask. You don't have to go behind my back.'

She took up his invitation in a totally unexpected manner. 'Have you ever killed an animal for sport?' The voice didn't sound like hers. It was as thin and hard as a sheet of ice.

Devlin froze under the chill of it. His angry eyes dropped from her pale, blank face to the album he now held. He opened it, even though he knew what he would find...

'Well, have you ever?' Her smile was a mockery of humour, her question unnecessary. The evidence was irrefutable, photograph after photograph of Devlin and male friends at various camps in various weathers with various kills, laughter and death inextricably mingled. All the men were smiling, proud of the destruction they had wrought, loving the sport of killing animals whose only mistake had been to seek to exist in the same world.

Devlin closed the padded book with a gentle finality, as if closing a chapter of his life. But it wasn't over, it could never be over. That chapter was part of what made him the man he was: the predator, the sleek and powerful bringer of death. She had likened him to a panther, but at least the panther never killed just for the pleasure of it!

'Cressy——'

He had lost her.

'No wonder you were so shocked to find out who I was,' Cressy said hoarsely, so pale that she looked like a haunting in the book-lined room, hushed with horror. 'You're a killer. You breed beautiful horses, but animals that can't be captured to serve your needs or contribute to your wealth you kill without care or conscience——' Her whisper was like a scream of pain in the silence.

'Cressy——'

'*Don't touch me!*' She recoiled from his hand. 'You're disgusting!' She drew a breath on a sob. 'Do you have any *conception* of the damage that men like you have done to the world? Do you even *care*? Of course you don't. You rape the land in the name of profit, and in the name of pleasure you destroy what's left!'

She didn't want to hear his apologia, his excuses. She had heard them all before. It slashed her to the bone to think of him parroting the same hackneyed self-serving phrases she had heard other hunters use. She struck aside his restraining hand and dashed out of the room, hot, bitter tears thawing the ice that had encased her when she had realised what he was.

She locked her door but she knew he wouldn't follow. What could he say in the face of such damning evidence? There was no defence for the indefensible. Her tears didn't ease the ache in her heart. She had been fooling herself. She hadn't run away this afternoon because she didn't trust him, but because she was afraid she did. He had cared for her, seen her at her worst, and still wanted her. Her clumsiness had evoked his tender amusement, not the usual male impatient irritation. He had been curious about her, and that in turn had evoked her own curiosity. He had flattered her with his desire, and the possessiveness that she sensed went against the grain of his nature. He had vowed never to be a slave to his father's obsession, but that vow had somehow spilled over into his private life, as if he had subconsciously decided that no object or person or interest must take such a hold on him that it would be impossible for him to give up. Hence the passing parade of women, the many different sports and interests. Only here, at Rush House, did he allow himself the luxury of pride of ownership. The stud was his, was something he would not be asked to give up. It was the home of his heart, however much he travelled, whatever trials he faced, personal or professional.

Cressy had no such home place, and yet with Devlin, for the first time, she had truly felt the lack of it, had envied him his sheet anchor, had wanted that stability for herself. That was why she had stayed. Not because of her lost gear, or her illness, although they were contributing factors, convenient excuses to hide behind. It was her need to get to know Devlin that had held her

captive, a deep-seated hunger to respond to the longings
of her bruised and wary heart, to rid herself of pervasive
self-doubt that had riddled all her previous relationships
with men, to persuade herself that this man was worthy,
despite their many differences, of all the love that was
dammed up inside her, aching for release. And this was
where her magnificent self-deception had led her: to pain
and disillusionment! He was no different from all the
others. And, more shatteringly to the point, *she* was no
different. Still incapable of a love that didn't blow up
in her face!

Well, crying over her foolishness wasn't going to help.
It wasn't her style. Her style was to chalk it up to experience and go on, and on, and *on* ... Cressy felt her
courage falter and she grimly donned the nun's habit
that Devlin had selected as fitting evening wear. If she
had been tired of the endless cycle of falling in and out
of love before Devlin, now she felt utterly exhausted.
Because she had the awful feeling that falling *out* of love
with him was going to be a hell of a lot more difficult
than the falling *in* had been. Not that she was really in
love, she told her reflection in the wicked mirror over
the bed. No. It was another illusion, another temporary
infatuation. She had always expected it to end badly,
and it had. She would just have to tough it out as usual.

She wished Devlin had seen fit to buy her some make-
up to go with the dress. She didn't wear it often, but
now she felt defenceless without it. When a woman was
down she needed to look good. Carmine lips and gold
eyelids might have made her feel real, not like a shadow
of her former self. She pinched her cheeks and bit her
lips and loosened her hair. More, she needed *more* ...
She took her comb and teased at her hair until it was a
fierce mane. Now she looked more like the way she felt,
like a stick of dynamite, a black sheath topped by a
burning red fuse.

When the knock came at her door the gaping holes in her defences were bristling with armour, but it was Frank who took a hasty step back as she flung it open.

'Uh—Devlin sent me up to get you. He wasn't sure you'd be down for dinner...'

'Why shouldn't I be?' she snapped.

'He—er—said you might be tired...after your ride.' Frank's brown eyes studied her tense figure.

'Did he?' Her voice was filled with a cool lack of interest that didn't fool him for a moment.

He shrugged. 'Actually he said a hell of a lot more, none of it repeatable to a lady. I take it you two have had another dust-up?'

He made it sound as if she and Devlin did nothing but fight, which wasn't far wide of the mark, come to think of it. Yet another reason why this attraction between them could come to no good. 'Didn't he tell you how I stranded him in the middle of nowhere, in the rain?' she said evasively.

Frank's mouth curved, his eyes twinkling suddenly. 'He might have mentioned something of the kind. I've been very tempted myself, on occasion. How did it feel?'

Cressy smiled unwillingly. 'Fantastic,' she admitted, and he laughed, tucking his arm through hers and turning her towards the stairs.

'I think his pride was dented. Devlin can be pretty touchy about his pride. I guess it stems from all the suffering he had to endure in his boyhood.'

Cressy's steps faltered. 'Suffering? I thought his parents were very happy together. The way he talks about this place I thought he had very affectionate memories of his childhood...' There, it was more of a comment than a question. If Frank chose to tell her anything it wouldn't be because she had *asked*...

'Oh, he does. He spent a lot of time here because his father travelled so much and Mariana—that's his mother—used to stay here instead of at their formal home in Auckland because she liked the countryside and

thought it was important for Devlin to have lots of fresh
air and freedom while he was young. She naturally
expected that Devlin would take over from Duncan one
day, there was no question that he would ever evade *that*
responsibility, but in the meantime she encouraged him
to live his own life—hence his rough-and-tumbling
around the world in his salad days. And he didn't let
them down; when they needed him back he came...'

'Doesn't sound much like suffering to me,' said Cressy,
struggling to control her fascination.

'No—I got a bit off-track there. You know, before he
acquired that scar, Devlin was bloody beautiful to look
at.' The Australian drawl was suddenly very pro-
nounced. 'We both went to the same school and Dev
was always getting into fights with kids who made the
mistake of thinking he was as pretty by nature as he was
by face. He was teased mercilessly about having an angel-
face. That's how he got his nickname; he played up like
the devil to make sure everyone knew he was as tough
as the next guy. In fact, that's how we became friends.
He punched me out for taunting him——'

'But you're younger than he is!' Cressy was shocked.
They had reached the downstairs hall but she lingered,
holding him back, wanting to hear the end of the story
before she braced herself to see the object of their discussion. 'You mean he picked on someone smaller than
himself?'

'I'm only three years younger. And I was a cocky little
brat in those days—the epitome of the snotty private-
school kid who thought he knew it all. And look at me!
Do I look as if I was ever puny? I was the bigger boy,
which is probably why I felt free to show off at Dev's
expense. We had a real ding-dong battle in the play-
ground—bloody noses, torn shirts... We both got sus-
pended for a week when neither of us would say who
started it.' He grinned. 'Much as Dev might hate to admit
it, one of the reasons the bullies steered clear of him
after that, other than his devil of a temper, was because

he had a great hulking Aussie for a friend! Of course there was a bright side to his gorgeousness too—he didn't half pull the birds, and naturally I benefited from the overflow. But it made him cynical about the superficial judgements people make. I won't deny that he's used his flattering looks to get his own way often enough, but he's never been narcissistic and I think that he's always secretly resented the indiscriminate nature of his advantage. Devlin doesn't like things to be too easy, or to be at the mercy of situations he can't control. I think he was actually relieved when he got that scar. Every time she sees him Mariana begs him to have plastic surgery but he won't hear of it. I think he enjoys the touch of menace it provides him with. Dev is a romantic at heart, though of course he'd never admit it——'

Cressy snorted. A romantic didn't go around with a gun killing defenceless animals. 'Did he ask you to tell me all this about him?' she said suspiciously. Was Frank supposed to be softening her up?

'No. And it's not the kind of personal information he likes to spread around,' Frank said, with a direct look that allayed her doubts. 'One way and another Dev's had to put up with a lot of intrusive publicity in his adult life but, again, all that stuff is pretty superficial; it glosses over a hell of a lot about the man in favour of the "once-over-lightly" attention-grabbing headlines. They've made him out to be a bit of a dilettante and that's one thing he's emphatically not. I thought it might help you understand him better to know that a lot of his apparent arrogance is hard-earned self-confidence——'

'Thanks, but I don't *want* to understand him better than I already do,' Cressy interrupted stiffly as they entered the lounge. It wouldn't do for Devlin to discover they were talking about him.

Frank had saved one, last disturbing comment. 'I have a feeling that what either of you want doesn't have a hell of a lot of bearing on what you're going to get . . .

Shall I escort you over to him?' Devlin was talking to David Eastman.

'No, thanks, Devlin and I have said everything we need to say to each other...'

'Cressy, whatever he said to you, bear in mind that he's under a lot of pressure here.'

'Oh? In what way?'

Frank looked vaguely uneasy, and patently relieved when Sir Edward Davies interrupted them.

'Well, Miss Cross, I suppose this is the last time we'll dine together. Are you going to have a relaxing sherry before dinner? Connell's got some very fine stuff.' He raised his own glass so that the light caught the pale straw-coloured liquid.

Cressy felt that she would need a barrel of the stuff to make her relax. 'Yes, I think I will.' As Frank wandered over to the drinks tray on the table to fulfil her request Cressy turned her attention full on Sir Edward. 'Did you say the last time?'

Sir Edward nodded his grey head. 'One more session in the morning to finalise our initial report and we'll all be off back to the real world, except Connell, of course— I understand you're staying on a few days. To tell you the truth I suspected this whole thing might be a waste of time, but that young man of yours has a power of determination; he knows how to motivate even die-hard old capitalists like us. I tell you, I'd far rather be dealing with him than some petty Government official, or some of those long-haired radicals who pass themselves off as "experts" on the environment. It's all very well for them to sound off about the sanctity of nature but, come to the crunch, it's a matter of human survival that we use the resources around us. Can't turn the clock back to the days of horses and carts and candles and hand-looms. We've outgrown all that as a species. We have to look forward, not back. That's something that Connell understands. He realises that the solutions to the world's problems have to come out of technology, out of the brain, not the heart.'

Now Cressy realised why so much secrecy had surrounded this meeting of industrial minds. From the frequent references to Devlin she gathered that he was not only hosting but chairing the meeting, and its purpose was now evident. These men were here as elected representatives of their respective industries, to discuss and formulate a collective environmental policy that would meet the concerns of the growing public disquiet about the wholesale destruction of the environment. Greenpeace and other similar groups had raised world consciousness to the point where it now made economic sense to heed the warnings. The industrialists evidently feared the effect of knee-jerk government reactions, especially during election years, just as much as they feared the adverse effects of changing public opinions and the actions of fanatical 'greenies'.

In her state of high tension, Cressy found her discovery exhilarating. How incredible that she should unknowingly be a witness to history in the making! This story could make a fortune for whoever broke it in the local media; in fact it would probably make an impact worldwide! But the temptation was only fleeting. She wasn't a journalist, and although her sympathies were firmly on the side of the environmentalists she was intelligent enough to see how fragile this coalition was, how vulnerable to outside pressures. From what Sir Edward had let slip, this was only the first of a whole series of think-tank meetings, and to broadcast its purpose now would be to torpedo any hopes of a consensus. Time enough for public input and debate later, when and if any kind of agreement was actually achieved.

Her exhilaration was tempered by puzzlement. The picture of Devlin as prime mover in all this didn't quite jell with her image of him as a mindless, bloodthirsty killer. On the other hand, the best huntsmen usually prided themselves on their 'responsibility' towards the animals they killed. Such men always tried to ensure a 'clean' kill, were careful to leave their campsites as pristine as when they had arrived, and often rebutted criticism by breeding pheasants or other game-birds to release into the wild in numbers that equalled their 'bag' for the year.

So caught up was she with her revealing conversation with Sir Edward that she didn't notice Devlin's approach until he took her lightly by the elbow with a murmured excuse to her companion and steered her towards the table. She had known that his eyes had been on her since she'd entered the room, but she had been proud of the fact that she hadn't looked at him once. He must have recognised her explosiveness, because he hadn't even attempted to approach her until now. The discussion with Sir Edward had taken some of the edge off her lethal anger, but she still vibrated with loathing as she moved stiffly away.

'I'm surprised you're still here,' Devlin commented in a low voice, nodding at Hugh Alton who had arrived late and was looking his customary brooding self.

Cressy stiffened further, pulling her arm out of his hand. 'What do you mean?'

He turned towards her, his shoulders blocking out her view of the rest of the room. 'Well, you think I'm such a contemptible swine, I'm stunned that you didn't just pack and storm out before you became contaminated by my blood-spattered home...'

Cressy stared at him blankly, not reacting to his dark sarcasm, her mind whirling. An arrested expression appeared on his face, his eyes narrowing.

'It never occurred to you, did it?' he breathed incredulously.

'W-what?'

The knowledge gripped him, taunted him with triumph on the wings of failure. 'To run from the Devil. To walk out in disgust. You hate what you think I am, but you can't run away from me. You'd rather stand and fight...'

'I ... you ... I don't have any transport,' Cressy floundered, shocked at the truth of his words. Shattered by his betrayal, she had still got dressed and come down to dinner, knowing she would see him. She had still *wanted* to see him, if only to reinforce her loving contempt, to wallow in her own martyred misery.

He smiled, a thin movement of his lips, his eyes as cold as bullets. 'That didn't stop you before. I don't doubt you could walk out the gates of hell if you were determined enough. You're a guest, not a prisoner here. If you wanted to leave, all you had to do was ask for it to be arranged. But you didn't even ask, did you, Cressy? Because you were afraid that it would be that easy...and that difficult. You didn't make the choice because you couldn't. Walking away from me unscathed is not an option any more. You might not trust me, but what we *feel* is much stronger and more important than any intellectual differences we might have——'

'I don't feel anything for you,' Cressy denied thickly, raising her hands in an ineffectual gesture to ward off his words as he came closer, his hard, lean body almost touching hers. But he made no attempt to touch her, except with his eyes.

'Do you know, Cressy, that the best way to get rid of a temptation is to yield to it?' he taunted huskily. 'If you try and resist it, the longing only digs deeper, grows stronger, until you're sick with desire for what you've cruelly forbidden yourself...'

The smoky words sounded vaguely familiar to her ears, or was it just that they struck a chord in her trembling heart? Cressy shook her head vaguely, unable to tear her eyes away from his, excruciatingly aware that he was seducing her in a roomful of people with his wicked words. She had accused him of having no conscience, and now she *knew* he had none. How could he talk like this, like a lover, when he knew how bright and fresh her bitterness burned?

'And do you know what the best defence against temptation is?' he went on, not waiting for her answer, his voice as soft and smooth as tearing silk. 'Cowardice.' His smile was filled with confidence as hers visibly wavered. 'What a pity, Cressy, that you don't have an ounce of it in your soul. So tough, so fierce...so brave...rushing clumsily in where angels—and devils— fear to tread. Shall we dine?' He drew back his body and her chair at the same time.

Sup with the Devil? The phrase popped unwillingly into her mind. Except that Devlin was inviting her to do more than merely sup; he wanted to feast, he wanted them to gorge themselves until temptation lost its potent lure and became just another passing experience to be added to his tally. Cressy sat down, her legs suddenly as weak as her will, her emotions in a turmoil. No, she wouldn't...couldn't betray her principles even for him. He obviously found it easy to compartmentalise his life: here business, here play; here lust, here respect. Cressy was not so organised; her life was an untidy tapestry of interdependent threads. When she loved it must be with the whole mind, the whole body, not just the expedient bits!

He made no further effort to speak to her as they dined, and for that she was grateful. What could she say? Cressy had never been very good at lying. As long as she stayed silent she was safe.

Her introspection made her even more clumsy than usual, and she was beginning to get quite embarrassed about the sidelong looks she was getting when she heard David Eastman say something about trout fishing in Taupo and then Sir Peter Hawthorne said, 'Didn't you have a fishing and hunting lodge at Taupo, Connell? Get down there much these days?'

'I still fish occasionally, but I don't hunt.'

Cressy dropped her fork, which fell on to the elegant white and gold bread and butter plate, cracking it neatly in half. She blushed furiously as Sir Peter sent her an irritated look.

'Why not? Lost the taste for it?'

It was an oblique challenge. Cressy would have had to have been blind and deaf not to have noticed that, of all those present, Sir Peter was the most persistently antagonistic towards his host. Whether it was personal, or whether it had to do with the group dynamics of the meeting, she wasn't sure.

'Yes. As a matter of fact I sold the lodge five years ago.'

Sir Peter was not so easily diverted. 'I'm a bit of a huntsman myself. Deer mostly. Didn't I read somewhere that you farm deer nowadays? Like fish in a barrel, I suppose?'

Cressy's hand clenched on the table-top. She was revolted by the jeering remark. She had heard stories of mindless morons who enjoyed taking pot-shots at penned deer from helicopters, sometimes with semi-automatic weapons. Surely Devlin wasn't involved in that kind of travesty of what had once passed for a noble blood-sport? She couldn't remain silent any longer. She opened her mouth to fling down her rage at the sickness of such ugly minds. Her breath choked in her throat as a big hand closed over her whitened knuckles, encompassing her hand completely.

Devlin didn't look at her as he addressed his guest evenly. 'I farm deer, yes, but experimentally, for stud purposes. If I wanted to hunt any animal I would at least allow it the chance of being hunted in its own natural environment, otherwise it seems rather a pointless exercise in self-gratification. As it is, I no longer get any personal satisfaction from hunting.'

'Changed your tune,' Sir Peter grunted. 'You used to be quite a gun, if you'll excuse the pun.'

The smiles around the table were few and tense, awaiting the blow-up. It didn't come.

'But not enough of one, apparently,' said Devlin calmly. 'It was reported in the Press at the time, but perhaps you weren't aware that my best friend was accidentally killed on a hunting expedition with me five years ago. It made me reassess my attitudes to life and death in general, and hunting in particular. It brought home to me in a very personal and forceful way that life is enough of a lottery without having the odds stacked against you. Whether you're man or beast, an unnecessary death is a wrongful death.'

There was an uneasy silence. Sir Peter was a very shrewd and aware man. There was no one present who doubted that he had known all along about the accident and had sought to goad Devlin into mentioning it as a sign of weakness. The opposite had proved true in the honest dignity of his answer.

Cressy was staring at the hand enveloping hers, Devlin's measured words sinking into her brain. Compassion flooded her thoughts, cleansing her spirit as she registered the unspoken pain that flowed beneath the surface of his rigid control. Such agony, such *feeling*...she felt it as if it were her own. His hand was so large, so capable, still bearing the scars and calluses of his trained profession, yet so gentle as it lay, warm and heavy, on hers, gently restraining her ready anger, quietly sharing it. She flexed her fingers experimentally and his curved protectively around them, loosely, so that she could withdraw without effort if she wished. She didn't. She could not bear to reject his pain. Her acquiescence was an unspoken apology, a public support. She owed him that much, at least. She had judged him blindly—with perfectly good reason perhaps, but still blindly. He had his vulnerabilities, like everyone else. He had made his mistakes...and paid for them in ways that she didn't yet comprehend. Would she ever fully understand this man? A tingling began low in her stomach, spreading a warmth throughout her body. Did she dare try?

CHAPTER SEVEN

'DEVLIN...do you *have* to keep turning away like that at the vital moment?'

'You told me to ignore the fact that you're here,' Devlin pointed out reasonably, removing Tussore's bridle, stroking the oiled silk neck as he crooned his approval of her performance over the jumps in the side paddock.

'I've photographed some shy animals in my time,' Cressy complained as she clicked the shutter again. 'But you make them look like extroverts. Do you think I'm trying to steal your soul with the film...?'

He turned to look at her then, his hand resting on Tussore's glossy hide. It was a striking shot—the strong, arrogant beauty of both man and horse sharply exposed in the harsh afternoon sunlight—and Cressy took it as Devlin said derisively, 'I thought you said you were an expert at candid shots.'

'I didn't say I wasn't getting what I wanted,' said Cressy, with an arrogance all of her own. 'Just that you're a difficult subject.' He seemed to be as physically elusive as he was mentally. Just when she thought she had him squarely in the frame he would slip out of focus. It had been like that for the last three days, ever since the meeting had broken up and the participants had been ferried by helicopter back to their respective empires. To Cressy's dismay, Frank had left with the others, leaving only Seiver as a truculent buffer between herself and the man whom she both loved and doubted with equal intensity. When she had weakly suggested hitching a ride on the final flight, Devlin had calmly proffered his bait: didn't she want to wait a day or two and capture the birth of Rain Lady's foal? And what about the shots

she had said she wanted of Devlin? Not only was he at
her disposal over the next few days, but he could even
provide her with the necessary darkroom facilities! He
had then taken her down to the previously unexplored
cellar of the house and shown her a small but very
modern, very expensively equipped and well-stocked
darkroom. She had been amazed and not a little disconcerted that he had gone to all that effort.

Cressy suddenly realised that she had taken several
shots on automatic pilot, without even being aware of
what she was doing. She glared at the subject of her
shots, and the cause of her distraction.

He raised his eyebrows. 'Now what have I done?'

'Nothing,' said Cressy hurriedly. Only invaded her
mind to the point where she could hardly think of anything, or anyone, else! She had been insane to stay on,
even if she had got some superb shots last evening of
Rain Lady producing her first foal—a toffee-coloured
filly with legs as thin and uncooperative as pick-up-sticks.
The mare had not had an easy labour and John Hewson,
Devlin and the vet had worked and worried for hours
in the muggy heat of the confined stall. Devlin had been
right in the thick of things, revealing an instinctive skill
in helping to calm and control the animal that had moved
Cressy by its naturalness. She had seen that Devlin's
painfully awakened reverence for life was deeply in-
stilled, enough to make him fight grimly against the odds,
even when he was exhausted, fearing the worst, his sweat-
soaked limbs wrenched and bruised by the frightened
threshing of Rain Lady's huge, heaving body. It had had
nothing to do with the value of the animal or its offspring and everything to do with preserving the miracle
of life. By the time the vet had pulled the reluctant foal
from its mother, all three men had stripped to the waist,
their chests and arms covered with sweat, dust and straw
and, in the case of the vet, blood. True to her word,
Cressy had made herself as small and unobtrusive as
possible, quietly taking her pictures, fascinated as much

by the masculine interplay as by their empathy with the distressed animal. When both mare and foal were out of danger Devlin had fetched a bottle of champagne from the stable fridge and they'd drunk it right there, toasting the victory. Cressy had taken a shot or two of their weary exhilaration before the vet had left and she had finally trudged off to bed, knowing that Devlin would probably remain in the stables for hours yet, keeping a quiet vigil with John to make sure there were no delayed complications. And this was the man who was still haunted by the five-year-old image of himself as a taker of life, rather than a giver.

Devlin had told her about the fatal hunting trip with his friend, Mark Alexander, at their first dinner alone together. His curiously blank tone had told her as much as the starkly laid out facts. He'd expected her to blame him as much as he blamed himself.

Although the police had been satisfied that the shooting had been totally accidental and there had been no carelessness involved, Devlin felt otherwise. Cressy had found no easy words of reassurance, for it was obvious that the knowledge that he was in any way instrumental in his best friend's death was a burden he would carry for the rest of his life. Mark had not been a particularly keen huntsman but he had accompanied Devlin on his trips because of their close friendship. The day the accident had occurred, Mark had elected to stay at the cabin while Devlin went out into the bush, tracking deer. But Mark had later changed his mind and followed Devlin, without bothering to change into the distinctive clothing they had both donned for hunting. It was not known exactly what happened in the bush, only that Mark's gun had fired accidentally, hitting him in the abdomen. Devlin had not returned to the cabin until some hours later, and by the time he had gone searching for his friend it had been too late.

'He was only thirty-two—younger than me—and had a gorgeous young wife he was madly in love with. They both trusted me. I knew Mark wasn't really comfortable with guns or the whole hunting ethic but he pretended to enjoy himself for my sake——' Devlin had broken off and taken a deep swallow from his glass of wine, forcing himself to go on. 'He didn't die immediately, you know. It took a while for the shock and blood-loss to take effect. For all the good my friendship did him then, I might as well have pulled that trigger myself.' Devlin's mouth had twisted in a way that had pulled his scar into prominence. 'Oh, intellectually I accept that accidents happen, that Mark was an adult and responsible for making his own decisions...and mistakes. But emotionally I know the ultimate responsibility was mine. I'd been selfish, and someone else had paid the price. I haven't picked up a gun since, and I never will again.'

Cressy had believed the quiet vow. She knew it must have taken a great deal of inner strength and courage to carry him emotionally intact through such an obviously turbulent period of remorse and personal self-doubt. It might have crippled a lesser man...or, worse, not changed him at all. Devlin accepted that his friend's death had diminished him, and had learned from the experience...

Cressy deliberately focused on an extreme close-up of Devlin's face as he stroked Tussore, ruefully noting the lack of physical evidence of his exhausting night in the stables. There were no creases of tiredness on his face, no flaws other than that sexy scar. She had had several solid hours of sleep and yet she still had dark circles under her eyes and a general grittiness of body and temperament that hadn't been banished by Devlin's offer at breakfast to let her photograph him after their regular morning ride. He had been patronising over her scratchiness, which had only annoyed her more and prompted her to draw out the session with some uncharacteristic messing about. It had felt good to order him ruthlessly around under the guise of professionalism.

'Smile at the birdie,' she demanded, with a reckless last-ditch effort to get under his sexy skin.

He obeyed meekly, beautifully, condescension reeking from every gorgeous, virile pore. Cressy gritted her teeth as she depressed the shutter. If there was anything worse than being laughed at, it was being *understood*! Was she really that transparent?

'OK, that's enough...for now, anyway.' She added the last because it seemed to be the only pitiable threat that she could brandish with Devlin in such an insufferably good mood.

He handed Tussore over to the stable boy and joined her just in time to stop her stepping into a convenient little mound of horse manure.

'You're in your element calling the shots, aren't you?' he mocked. 'As long as you're holding that camera in your hand you don't make one mistake. You never stumble or falter——'

'Why should I? I've trained for years to achieve a high standard of professionalism. It's not just a matter of pointing the camera and clicking.'

'I know that. I wasn't questioning your skill. What I meant was that you're in total control of yourself when you're working, totally uninhibited in your single-mindedness and yet totally co-ordinated...graceful, in fact. Just as you are when you're in a rage. It's only when you don't have anger or a viewfinder to concentrate your energies through that you knock things over and walk into walls—all right, that's a slight exaggeration, but you know what I mean! I don't think you do those things because you're naturally clumsy, but because most of your self-control is burnt up in your headlong pursuit of artistic excellence. You couldn't sustain that kind of concentration all the time without collapsing from mental exhaustion, so your natural co-ordination elects to take a holiday when you do...'

'Oh, you know me that well, do you, after only a week?' Cressy said sourly, to hide her frank dismay. Yes, obviously she *was* that transparent. What else did he know about her?

'Time has nothing to do with it,' he said gently, attuned to her faint tension. 'You can be friends with someone all your life and never really understand how they think or feel. You can meet someone once and instinctively know that they have some deep connection with your private inner self that cuts across the normal polite social barriers... like you and me.'

'As I remember it, we were instant enemies,' said Cressy tartly, wiping her shoes on the back doormat while Devlin used the boot scraper. 'I thought you were a murdering tyrant, you thought I was a spy!'

'Your memory of that occasion isn't exactly reliable,' he pointed out. 'Besides, although I'm no longer an avid churchgoer I was brought up according to the Good Book. I was always taught that to achieve salvation one must learn to love one's enemies... do you think you can teach me to do that, little saint?'

'You're way beyond salvation, Devlin Connell,' Cressy said loudly, to drown out the thunder of her heart. Was he really talking of love... or merely lust? Did he know the difference? Did she care? She already knew that the charming Devil wasn't as black as he had been painted, but she was no saint herself, not with the thoughts that were flitting through her head right at this moment!

'Surely you couldn't be so cruel as to deny a poor sinner at least the chance of redemption, Cressy, darling?' he continued in a voice as thick and sweet as honey. Oh, he was tempting, but Cressy was made of sterner stuff. She clutched her camera tightly.

'Perhaps you ought to try a little more praying and a little less baying,' she said nastily, and after a stunned second he began to laugh. He looked marvellous, standing on the doorstep in his riding gear, hands on hips, head thrown back in amusement, a picture of reckless masculine confidence. Cressy forgot she'd used the last of her film and was raising her camera again when the door whipped open behind her, nearly toppling her backwards.

'Phone!' Seiver snarled, offended by the levity on his doorstep. The security men and their dogs had been dispatched along with the guests, but with Seiver around Cressy hardly noticed the Alsatians had gone, he did such a good job of bristling and barking. Actually, the Alsatians had been friendlier!

Devlin stepped automatically forward. 'Oh, good, is it Frank?'

'Not for you. For her.' Seiver jerked a thumb in Cressy's direction. 'For Crash.'

Cressy winced as Devlin frowned. 'What did you call her?'

'Not me, the dame on the phone,' said Seiver smugly. 'Asked to speak to "Crash Cross". Said that's what everyone calls her.'

'Only my friends,' said Cressy darkly, as Devlin erupted into fresh laughter.

'Oh, and what do your enemies call you?'

'Ma'am.' She put her nose in the air and stalked into the house.

It was Nina, checking to see that she hadn't got 'lost in the bogs' as she put it and passing on a few messages—including one from her father who was apparently now in Turkey—none of which were really urgent. What Nina was really after was the hot gossip on the fascinating Devlin Connell.

'Fallen in love with him yet?' Here was another person who knew her too well for comfort...

'Nina——'

'OK. Scrub that. Gone to bed with him yet?'

'Nina!' She hoped to heaven that Devlin wasn't listening in to this call.

'Oh, I forgot, you can't have the other without the one, in your book. You're too much of a perfectionist, honey. He's gorgeous and loaded, what more could you ask? Oh, I know he doesn't look like a chipmunk or a

red panda or all the usual nice cutesy herbivores you go
for, but I would have thought you'd learnt your lesson
by now! Don't you ever hunger for a nice bit of carni-
vore? Bet Connell's got an appetite and a half, and for
red meat at that, so you've got a head start——'

'Nina!' Cressy was scarlet by now, having picked up
the phone in the hall in all innocence. She should have
remembered that Nina liked to be even more outrageous
on the phone than she was in person and she had a very
carrying voice. Devlin was now standing in the kitchen
doorway, observing with interest. 'I have no personal
interest in Devlin Connell,' she hissed indistinctly,
without moving her lips. 'And did you have to ask for
me by that stupid nickname?'

She bit off her remark as Devlin began to saunter
towards the stairs, watching her shoulders hunch further
with each step.

'You mean Crash? It just slipped out—sorry.' Her
friend was cheerfully unrepentant. 'Does that mean they
haven't discovered it for themselves yet? You *must* be
on good behaviour down there. No wonder you're niggly.
And you say you're not interested in Connell——'

'I'm not! For goodness' sake, keep your voice down!'
Cressy whispered frantically as Devlin stopped alongside her. Cressy straightened, glaring at him, and said
starkly, 'You'd better watch what you say, he's standing
right here. He has no respect for people's privacy. You
know, he listened in on the extension when I rang you
the first time——'

'No kidding? The sly devil!' Nina was admiring rather
than offended, her voice louder than ever. 'I hope he
was flattered. By people's privacy I presume you mean
your own. What does he do, follow you around?'

He had definitely heard that question, in spite of the
receiver being clamped against Cressy's skull, because
his eyes glowed with amusement at her predicament.
Cressy retaliated. 'Like a lost puppy!' she said
disparagingly.

'Puppy!' Nina's screech penetrated her ear-drum. 'My dear girl, Connell's been called a few names in his time but never a *dog*...a stallion, maybe!'

Cressy would have hung up, but Devlin deftly removed the receiver from her rigid grasp with a clever movement that left her nursing a numb wrist.

'Nina...? Yes, yes...more than flattered. No...yes...oh, I'm quite adequately insured, thank you, I think I'm in line to gain more than I lose. Oh, I have every intention of doing so. Yes...yes...standing here with her mouth open, blushing like a virgin...oh, really? Well, that's certainly very helpful to know...' Cressy was appalled at what she suspected the free-thinking, free-speaking Nina was telling him about her and made a grab for the phone. Devlin turned his back and her blow merely glanced off his powerful shoulders. He continued to easily parry her efforts as the rest of his half of the agonisingly long conversation—all of a few minutes—went on in the same vein...a lot of nerve-racking half-finished lines and tantalising phrases, and violently leading personal questions that he had no right to ask, let alone receive answers to. The only reason Cressy didn't storm off was because she feared that the conversation would get even more frank if she weren't here to monitor it. When Devlin finally handed back the telephone Cressy was furious with both of them.

'Thanks a lot, friend,' she said tightly.

Nina suddenly dropped her cheerful brashness. 'Hey, if I thought he was bad news I would have been a clam. You can't kid a kidder, honey. If you two are at each other's throats it's not because you want to rip them out! I was going to ask you when you think you'll be back, but I guess I'll expect you when I see you, huh? Which I guess from the tenor of the conversation is not going to be all that soon...'

She was still brooding over the embarrassing call hours later. At dinner she took Devlin severely to task for hijacking her personal phone calls. They were seated at one end of the enormous polished dining table, alone in intimate splendour, the soft light from the candelabra and the elaborate silver table-setting unnerving her almost as much as Devlin's dark, amused regard. He was totally relaxed; Cressy was all nerves, half expecting him to pounce any moment. And yet all he did was *talk* . . .

'I wanted to introduce myself,' he said mildly. 'Reassure her about my intentions. Your flatmate obviously worries about you.'

Cressy coughed into her wine. Maybe he hadn't heard what Nina had been yelling about after all!

'She's obviously concerned about your hopeless romantic gullibility. She thinks you ought to adopt a more practical approach to falling in love to compensate for your poor judgement. I told her I was hoping to teach you a little discrimination . . .'

It was a struggle, but Cressy managed to find the breath to say lightly, with just the right hint of amused scorn, 'You mean it would be good judgement to fall in love with someone like you?' She paused for the lightning strike, but it never came. Maybe lying by implication wasn't covered in the list of culpable sins. 'I'm not *that* much of a hopeless romantic!'

'You think falling in love with me would be a mistake?'

'The biggest!' said Cressy firmly.

'Why?'

She looked at him blankly. 'Why? There are so many reasons I can't begin to tell you.' For the moment she couldn't think of a single, solitary one. She settled for blurting nonsensically, 'Because we're obviously not suited, that's why.'

'None of the men you *thought* were suitable candidates for your loyal affections turned out to be. So why not try someone patently unsuitable? You might surprise yourself.'

'No, thanks. You may think I go around asking for trouble, but I don't go begging for it!'

For once she was relieved by Seiver's appearance, but when he put her chilled soup down in front of her she stared at it in surprise. It was served in a colourful plastic bowl. She looked over at Devlin's plate. His was an elegant gold-rimmed piece from the large, beautiful German dinner set which passed as a wealthy man's everyday crockery. She looked at Seiver. He was leering at her. Well, it was more of an expectant grin, really.

'I suppose you think this is hilarious,' she said sourly.

'I call it being practical, missy.'

What was it with people wanting to be practical all the time? It was so humiliating. 'Don't call me missy. I have a name, you know,' she said sharply.

Seiver shrugged with a suspicious lack of annoyance. 'OK. Just being practical—Crash.'

'She does have another name, Seiver,' Devlin commented, springing quickly to her defence—or so she thought! 'Her flatmate told me that she's also called Crosspatch; only at certain times, you understand.' They both looked at Cressy's sweetheart face, creased with a menacing scowl, the Cupid's bow mouth drawn into a stiff crinkle, the narrowed eyes the colour of ground pepper—or buckshot! The effect was predictable.

'Ho, ho, ho,' Cressy echoed their laughter hollowly. Nina *must* have been impressed. She had obviously bared all. Nothing like being abandoned by your friends to make you feel confident. 'I suppose I should be grateful to you for not serving my wine in a baked bean tin.'

'I didn't want to embarrass you by being too obvious,' said Seiver piously. Cressy took careful aim with the buckshot.

'What is it with you and women, Seiver? Do you object to females personally, or just on general principle? You ought to come out of the closet if that's what's making you so testy.'

'Why, you little——'

Cressy stood up and thrust her face into his. 'Watch who you're calling little!'

'Wanna make somethin' of it?'

'Yeah!'

'Yeah?'

'Soup's getting cold!'

Ingrained manners had Cressy sagging back automatically into her seat before she realised how ridiculous the comment was.

'It's gazpacho,' she pointed out, looking at the ice-cubes floating in the tomato-based soup.

'Mmm, and delicious it is, too.' Devlin was eating with relish, totally unconcerned by the potential punch-up that had been brewing. 'Seiver learnt his trade in the Navy, you know. If his cooking was always this good it's a wonder there wasn't a mutiny when he left. He may be a bit cranky, but a man who can elevate cooking to the level of performance art is entitled to a bit of temperament, wouldn't you say, Cressy? What do you think of the gazpacho?'

Cressy knew even before she tasted it what she thought. Seiver wouldn't win any prizes for personality but he certainly made up for the presentation with the content. 'It's terrific,' she admitted reluctantly, then sighed and gave him his due. 'But then it always is. Did you really learn to do this sort of stuff in the Navy? I would have thought that hash-slinging for hundreds of men at a time wouldn't have given you time for developing any flair or frills.'

'We're talking modern Navy here.' Seiver unbent a little. 'Those boys like a bit of variation, something to talk about, while they're cooped up at sea. And then there's the top brass, they like to figure themselves gourmets.'

'Why did you leave?'

'Wife got sick. Had to stay home and look after her. When she died I didn't figure I wanted to go back. Got a job with Devil here. That was fifteen years ago. Been with him ever since.'

'Do you have any children?' murmured Cressy, feeling terrible now at having taunted him the way she did.

Seiver grinned at her, this time his eyes positively twinkling with repressed glee. 'Yeah. Five grown-up daughters. So ya see, missy, I seen enough of women to know when one is born to trouble. And I sure ain't gay!'

He was cackling as he left the room, his pigeon chest puffed out at getting such a satisfactory last word.

'I guess I have to resign myself to eating off plastic for the rest of my stay. Maybe it's for the best, anyway,' Cressy said wryly.

'He was just having you on. I think he likes you, in his own inimitable, insulting way. He knows we can afford the breakages—as I told your friend, I'm well insured. He's right about one thing, though: you're certainly born to trouble.'

She had known he would feel this way after the first bloom of challenge wore off, so why was she so disappointed? 'I know my clumsiness infuriates people——'

'I'm not talking about that. I happen to find your air of distraction very reassuring. You have intelligence, talent, confidence and a body that could—and did—stop conversation in a roomful of men. If you didn't have an endearing flaw or two you could be a very dominating woman.'

'Me?' Because she was short Cressy had never thought herself as being able to dominate anyone, physically or otherwise.

'Yes, you. Perhaps intimidating might be a better word. You have a very strong self-image. Nina says that's why you attract so many selfish lightweights as potential lovers. They're attracted by your strength and your passion and your instinct to love and cherish those you care about, but they can't cope with the discovery that for all your dashing modern air you have a good old-fashioned need to be cherished equally in return. You'll only give yourself fully to a man who can match you for tenderness as well as passion——'

'Are you saying I wanted to *mother* them?' Cressy
tried to fathom his complex reasoning.

He shrugged. 'Perhaps you confused what you needed
with what you wanted. The hunt for the right mate in-
volves us all in the tedious process of elimination. Not
many people find their ideal first time up. The trick is
not to let yourself get discouraged, and not to get misled
by the clever imitations. You trusted all those men you
fell for, I presume?'

'Of course. You can't have love without trust.'

'If only it were that convenient,' he murmured drily.
'Do you find me attractive, Cressy?'

She wished she could deny it, but they both knew dif-
ferently. 'You know I do,' she said sullenly. 'So what?'

'And do you trust me?'

Was he kidding? Trust the Devil? 'No further than I
could throw you!'

Instead of looking discouraged he leaned back with a
wicked satisfaction. 'There you are, then. At least I'm
nothing like your failures of the past. That's rather en-
couraging, don't you think?'

'That's the most ludicrous piece of double-think I ever
heard!' Particularly since it made a kind of horrifying
sense.

Just as Cressy braced herself to resist any further con-
fusing blandishments, Seiver came in with the main
course—stuffed trout in a luscious sauce—and dished
up Cressy's on to a large plastic platter. This time she
didn't utter a word and Seiver smirked at her dignified
silence. When he left the room Devlin suddenly began
to ask her some surprisingly technical questions about
her photography.

'You almost sound as if you know what you're talking
about,' she said, hiding her chagrin at the abrupt cur-
tailment of their verbal fencing.

'I enjoy using a camera. Nothing in your class, of
course, but I like to keep a visual record of life. People

talk about memories being vivid but so many good ones are lost in the shuffle...'

'You took a lot of the ones in those albums, didn't you?' said Cressy, remembering the large number of shots in which Devlin didn't feature.

He grinned, a trifle cockily she thought, remembering something else...

'Yeah. What did you think?'

'Well...' She pretended to think, and then leaned her elbow on the table and drawled slowly, 'What I think is, Devlin...is that you...take the very *worst* photographs of anyone I know!' His face fell comically and she laughed. 'Professionally speaking, they're terrible. You must be all thumbs with a camera.'

He rubbed his scar. 'I told you I wasn't in your class,' he said, his eyes the colour of a lowering sky.

'But you enjoyed taking them and looking at them, that's all that matters, Devlin.' She leaned over to pat his hand, sorry now that she had meanly rubbed his nose in his ineptitude. 'It doesn't matter about things like composition or frame when you're just taking pictures for fun. Who cares if it's slightly out of focus or there's a thumb covering a corner of the shot, as long as you get the memory you want?'

He grinned sheepishly, turning his hand to capture hers, some of his arrogance returning at her attempt to minister to his wounded ego. She had been teasing him, but she had also paid him an oblique compliment with her honest response. If she had been indifferent to him she might have politely lied. She had relied on him to be confident enough about himself to weather her frank criticism.

'And better a shot from a camera than a gun.'

'Yes,' she said soberly, knowing from the brief shadow in his eyes that he was thinking of Mark Alexander.

'Not that I've given up hunting entirely...'

Cressy stiffened, drawing back until his hand tightened, not noticing the glint in his eye.

He leaned into her withdrawal, his free hand coming up to stroke lightly down the side of her face, and up again. 'I read a poem, once, that expressed the nature of the sport perfectly:

'"Man is the hunter; woman is his game: the sleek and shining creatures of the chase, we hunt them for the beauty of their skins..."'

He watched the colour bloom gently where he touched, as if his trailing fingers were stirring strawberries into whipped cream. It ripened into a blush when he impulsively tasted his fingertips, curious to know if she tasted as good as she felt. She did.

'Well, I have no intention of being a trophy on anyone's wall,' Cressy said shakily. 'That's a very sexist poem.'

'But apt, in this case,' he murmured, replacing his fingers, aroused by the contrast of dark masculinity against pale femininity. 'Your beautiful skin was one of the first things I noticed about you...it's the same delicious creamy velvet all over. The only trace of colour is the tiny row of freckles down the length of your spine...don't you ever sunbathe?'

'With this horrifying hair?' Cressy said faintly, tingling at the knowledge that he had studied her so minutely, hypnotised by his evident, almost voluptuous pleasure in touching her.

'It's not horrifying, it suits you perfectly. I like the way it sizzles against your pale skin...' His finger was now tracing the demure neckline of her black dress.

'I used to hate being teased about it...' Cressy was hardly aware of what she was saying. Seiver had walked into the room at some stage, plonked the dessert down in front of them with a disapproving grunt and stomped out again. Neither of them had even noticed. 'Then I gave up fighting it and decided to flaunt it, instead.'

'Like a blazing banner of defiance.' He understood perfectly. He wore his scar with much the same deliberate contempt for opinion, as a mark of pride. His finger dipped below the neckline of her gown into the cleft between her breasts and she shivered and pressed her hands to her chest, trapping him there.

'Don't you like me touching you?'

'I thought this dress was supposed to discourage that sort of thing,' she said breathlessly. 'Frank said that you were very explicit in your instructions about what kind of dress to get for me. It had to be black and there had to be plenty of it. He said he thought it made me look like a nun.'

Devlin smiled, leaving his hand in its warm fleshy nest, quite content to have her think she was restraining him rather than arousing him further. 'A very provocative nun. I didn't want Eastman getting any ideas. Or Frank, for that matter.'

'You thought I might be attracted to Frank?' Cressy's eyes widened. When Devlin was about she hardly noticed any other men.

'He's more your age.'

'What's that got to do with it?'

It was on the tip of his tongue to remind her about her taunt that thirty-five was over the hill, but he didn't want to take the risk. Nor did he want to get into a discussion of the merits of youth versus experience. He would rather show her. 'I was just trying to cover all the bases,' he said smoothly.

'You mean all of me,' said Cressy, knowing she should be annoyed rather than flattered.

'I didn't want anyone to see you the way I had seen you. I didn't want anyone else counting the little freckles on your spine. They're a small secret shared between the two of us...'

'I didn't even know about them myself,' Cressy whispered. How had he got so close? His breath was warm against her lips.

'You see... I know you even better than you know yourself,' he said softly. 'I know, for instance, that you want me to kiss you like this...'

He moved his mouth the few millimetres necessary and suited the action to the words. He tasted of wine and warmth and an indefinable flavour that excited her unbearably. He cupped a big hand behind her head, weaving hard fingers into her hair, holding her still so that his tongue could move deeply inside her, filling her mouth, her senses, with pleasure. Her hands left their protective position at her breast and rose to his shoulders, feeling the heavy muscles shift as he leaned even closer, his knees bumping against hers before snugly sliding either side of her thighs, drawing her legs together and towards the centre of his body. He lifted his mouth and uttered a soft groan of pleasure as her knees pressed against his hardness.

'And I just know you want me to touch you like this...' The hand on the back of her head tunnelled under her hair and lightly stroked the nape of her neck. He was kissing her again as the back of her dress split open, the zip gliding down with soundless ease, and then he was stroking her bare skin, lingering briefly on the lacy strap that hindered his downward progress. That, too, silently gave way and his warm, callused palm was cupping her lower spine, arching her so that he could free the fabric from her full breasts. His kisses became soft, butterfly brushes against her mouth, her eyes, her jaw and throat as he peeled back the lace cups of her loosened bra. He stroked the lush sloping curves in a delicate, sweeping, circular motion that gentled her towards the desire for deeper intimacy as her neglected nipples ached for the same exquisitely delicate caress. By the time he touched them they were swollen and tight, agonisingly sensitive, so that the lightest brush of his thumb drew forth a sinful gush of delight. His fingers curled around the dark rose crests, possessing her completely, his eyes blazing with silvery sexual heat as he drank in the picture of passionate abandonment she presented, framed in his arms, mistress of his desire, slave to her own. He knew exactly how to tease out her arousal, milking her of pleasure with a slow, erotic rhythm, swallowing her little throaty moans with sips of his wickedly sensuous mouth. It was only when Cressy felt his hand on her bare knee, sliding up under the soft folds of her full skirt to dip between her silky thighs that she felt the first flicker of unease. He felt her tense, and murmured something against her mouth, and moved the V of his body insistently against her legs, impressing her with the heat and potency of his arousal, his readiness to increase her pleasure beyond imagining. The knowledge grew painfully, in that tiny part of her mind that was still capable of coherent thought, that she loved him too much to allow him a casual sexual victory. If she allowed Devlin to possess her once, he would possess her forever, long after his self-confessed hunting instinct had led him on to fresh prey. Her imagination suddenly visualised the empty future with a terrible, chilling clarity. If she couldn't hold him, she couldn't let herself have him at all...

'Devlin, no...'

With a clever twist of his hips he had insinuated himself between her knees so that she was clamping him intimately and the hand between her thigh was creeping inexorably higher, stroking her teasingly as it went.

'Devlin, *no*...!' His mouth closed over her breast and he suckled hotly, eyes watching her helpless pleasure, drawing them both deeper into the sensual lair where he could devour her completely.

'You can't deny it now, you know it's what you want,' he told her, in a harsh, husky voice that was almost a guttural growl. 'You want to feel me hard inside you... you want to draw me in and make me part of you... you want it so much you *can't* say no...'

For some reason her fevered mind latched on to the popular drug slogan. It was a lifeline. Devlin was like a drug, running hot and violent in her veins, and, like a drug, the dangerous toxins would remain long after the mind-blowing effects had passed. 'Just Say No.' That was all she had to do. *'Just Say No'*.

'Devlin, please...I can't...I don't...please don't make me...' Panic overwhelmed her as she couldn't frame the simple word and Cressy was shocked to feel her eyes filling with helpless tears. But no more shocked than Devlin. He froze, the flushed wildness of his expression dying to a grey sheen as he stared at the drop of moisture that had fallen on to her bare breast.

'Tears?' He sounded as stricken as she felt, speaking in jerky spasms. 'My God, Cressy, you can't be crying! You can't think I'd force you against your will? I want to make love with you, not rape you...'

But he didn't, that was the shame of it. What he wanted to do to her had as little to do with love as it had with the brutal act of rape. Still, he had good reason to look shocked, since up until now she had been with him every step of the way. Cressy wiped away her stubborn tears and struggled to hold up her dress.

'I...I'm sorry...I really am...I didn't mean...I think I feel sick——'

And she rushed out of the room, leaving the Devil in total disarray behind her.

CHAPTER EIGHT

'NORMALLY your stuff would have to be retained by the police until the trial, but since the evidence forms a vital part of your livelihood, Miss Cross, we can record it on videotape and release it to you within the next day or so. You'll have to fetch it from Hamilton police station, though...'

Cressy fiddled with the cord on the telephone in Devlin's office as she listened to Constable James Farradon tell her that the three young men who had stolen her car had merely intended to joyride to Hamilton, but the temptation of discovering thousands of dollars' worth of camera gear had proved too much and their opportunism had resulted in their being caught in a police operation against a property fencing ring. Cressy made the appropriate murmurs of gratitude but all she could think of was, Now what convenient excuse will I have to stay?

She found herself staring at one of Max's photographs as she put down the phone. Max took life by the throat and throttled every scrap of enjoyment out of it. He was as much an emotional risk-taker as a physical one. On the other hand, he was also the complete professional. Get the job done, then have your fling, that would probably be his advice. But what if she wanted more than a fling?

'Thinking about running away again, Cressy?'

'W-what?'

Devlin was leaning in the open doorway, arms folded across his chest. He wore riding gear, a fact which mocked her as much as his tone. She hadn't had the nerve to join him for their ride this morning. Even now

131

she could feel herself blush at the memory of what they had done last night, and what they hadn't . . .

'That *was* James, wasn't it?'

'Eavesdropping again, Devlin?' she mimicked his derision.

'This time I didn't have to. James rang last night, after you'd gone to bed, with the good news. In the circumstances I didn't think you'd want to be disturbed, so I suggested he call back this morning.'

'Oh.' His equable smile unnerved Cressy even more. How could he do that—mention last night without so much as a tinge of colour in his face or voice? 'He said I could sign some release papers and pick my things up in Hamilton . . .'

'So?' He remained at the door, yet Cressy felt he had just taken a giant step into the room.

'So . . . I suppose I need to do that . . .'

'You only suppose?'

For an equable man he was making this very difficult. Cressy looked down and found her hands tightly twisted together. She pulled them apart and put them behind her back, nervously gripping the polished edge of the desk as she leaned on it. Before she could speak, he did.

'Are you waiting for me to beg you to stay?'

'No!' That would be admitting how much she wanted him to! 'No, of course not. I was just wondering how to get there . . .'

'Ah. I see. You want me to provide you with the means to run away.'

'Will you stop *saying* that? I am *not* running away. I have a job to do, if you'll remember, on Middle Island.'

'The nature reserve—yes, I remember. Or is it called a sanctuary? That would be more appropriate, wouldn't it? You seem to spend your whole life seeking remote little sanctuaries where all the uncomfortable complexities of human emotions can be ignored——'

'If you're implying that I use my job as a kind of crutch, you couldn't be more wrong——'

'Is that what you think I'm implying?'

Oh, he was a clever devil, getting her to condemn herself out of her own mouth! She took a deep breath. 'Just because I don't want to fall into bed with you——'

'Don't you?' His look of amused surprise was the last straw. Of *course* she wanted to fall into bed with him, and he knew it, damn him! The pressure inside her skull heated up to exploding-point.

'Devlin——!'

'When do you want to leave?'

'*What?*'

'Seiver can drive you, but it'll be quicker by helicopter.'

All the fight sagged out of her. 'Y-you mean, you'll help me go?' she stammered, devastated.

He shrugged. 'I wouldn't dream of keeping you against your will. That's not what I want. Well...' His mouth curved suddenly, the silver eyes warming her pale frigidity. 'I might dream, but fantasies are never as satisfying in the long term as healthy reality.'

In the long term? 'Then what *do* you want?' she asked, her voice husky with caution.

'For you to feel comfortable with me.'

Comfortable? He had to be kidding!

He smiled at her shock. He flexed his shoulder and pushed himself away from the door, moving into the room with his hands thrust safely into the slim pockets of his jodhpurs. He kept his distance, circling around her wary figure until he was behind the desk, then he sat down, further diminishing the threat of his masculinity.

'I know you have a job to do, Cressy, and I appreciate the demands it makes on you. I wouldn't ask you to forgo your commitments on my behalf any more than I would expect you to ask me to forget my business obligations. But the two aren't necessarily incompatible. Where do you plan to go after you've done your giant wetas?'

'Nowhere immediately,' she said uncertainly. 'I mean, I have one or two things in the pipeline and a couple of long-term projects——' There was that tantalising word again. 'Long-term'.

'Oh? And what are they?'

She found herself telling him, and relaxing slightly in the telling. This was familiar territory.

'It sounds as if you can more or less create your own deadlines, within the timetable of the seasons,' he mused, putting his finger exactly on the things she most liked about her career—its flexibility, scope and freedom. 'Do you allow yourself the same leeway in your personal life? Are you prepared to give it the kind of devoted patience that you give your animal subjects? I'd like to know, Cressy, whether you're going to give up on us just because we both have jagged edges that don't quite accommodate each other...'

'I... what are you asking?'

He was quite as cautious as she, but from different motives entirely. 'That you don't vanish into the safety of your wilderness just yet. That you give me time to——' He paused delicately and she rushed recklessly in.

'Seduce me?'

He tilted his head back, resting it against a wing of the chair, smiling at her through narrowed eyes. 'I thought I'd already done that,' he said throatily, and she flushed. He grinned. 'Have a little faith, Cressy.'

'In you?'

'In yourself. I'm different from all the others, remember? Maybe this time your instincts are right.'

'My instinct is to run like hell,' said Cressy wryly.

His lids hooded the predatory silver eyes. He was fighting a fierce inner battle with his own primitive instinct to take what he wanted and worry about consequences later. But not hurting Cressy was almost as important, he had discovered, as having her. He would have her willingly or not at all. For the first time he

wished that his retirement were already a fact and that
he had the leisure to enjoy a prolonged game of 'will
she, won't she?' but the current pressures on him pre-
cluded that luxury. Next year perhaps... but he couldn't
wait that long, and he doubted Cressida would either.
Next year he would be forty. It was a landmark enough
to pass without having to pass it alone. He had never
imagined, in the flush of arrogant youth, that he
wouldn't be married by his fortieth birthday, surrounded by a wife and children whose demands and interests would naturally expand to fill the hole left by his
withdrawal from the corporation, his 'retirement to stud'
as Frank jokingly called it. The joke had palled because,
although Devlin had never felt sufficiently strongly about
any of the women in his life to settle with any particular
one, he had long since discovered that, if variety was
the spice of life, it also led to jaded tastebuds. He lived
in a world of money and power, both powerful aphro-
disiacs in themselves, attracting a certain kind of woman.
It was rare that a dewy-fresh wild flower like Cressy ever
turned up among the hot-house blooms that he had
become used to. More than rare—unique.

'That's your first instinct. What's your second?' he
asked softly, and was delighted to see her blush. 'Mine,
too,' he murmured and watched her little chin lift
haughtily, the kissable bow of her mouth tightening into
a hard knot.

'My second instinct is to smack that smug leer off
your face,' she denied sharply.

He laughed and stood up, coming around the desk
towards her. 'Be my guest, Cressy.' He picked up her
clenched hand and unfolded it against the scarred side
of his face, holding it there so that she could feel the
thin ridge pressing into her palm, the smooth hardness
of his jaw against the base of her thumb, the textured
firmness of his temples against her fingers. His pulse
beat against the tip of her ring finger, making her simultaneously aware of his human fragility and his ag-

gressive vitality. The pulse quickened as she stared at
him and the silver eyes darkened, the pupils widening
until only a thin silver rim surrounded the velvety
blackness. His skin heated beneath her touch and he
turned his mouth and bit softly into the padded base of
her thumb that rested against his jaw. His teeth gripped
her lightly while his tongue stroked. She trembled and
he whispered against her stinging flesh, 'I have a tough
hide, Cressy, but that's all it is—an outer skin. You could
hurt me if you wanted to, though not by hitting. Would
you like to make me suffer, because of what I've made
you feel?'

The door rattled and Seiver stomped in with his usual
surly disregard for their privacy. Cressy had never been
more glad of an interruption in her life.

'That woman's back,' he told Devlin glumly.

Devlin jerked away from Cressy as if she had suddenly been declared a quarantine risk. *'Gianetta?'*

Seiver nodded. 'That woman,' he confirmed flatly.

Devlin swore under his breath and turned to Cressy.
He started to speak, then hesitated. He walked to the
door and hesitated again before hurrying out with a brief
exclamation of impatience.

It was a moment before Cressy could bring herself to
move. 'That woman' had an ominously familiar ring to
it, and Devlin's indecision seemed unaccountably guilty.

'Where do you think you're going?' said Seiver,
stepping in front of her as she reached the door.

'Out,' said Cressy, unrevealingly.

He grinned smugly at her. 'You'll be sorry!'

Cressy knew he was baiting her but she couldn't help
snapping. 'Why? Who is she?'

'Gianetta Alexander. An old friend, she *calls* herself...'
Seiver snorted sceptically.

The name rang distant bells. 'No relation to Devlin's
friend who was killed—Mark?'

'His widow,' said Seiver. 'The Black Widow, I call
'er.'

'He was younger than me and had a gorgeous wife'...
Cressy recalled the words with crystal clarity. She looked
down at herself. Jeans and plain white blouse and
sneakers weren't exactly the height of elegance, but she
had the sinking feeling that she wasn't going to be able
to compete anyway.

Her first glimpse of Gianetta Alexander was
daunting—a very slender, sexy back swathed in blue
crêpe de Chine and wrapped in male arms—Devlin's
arms. They weren't kissing but they evidently had been,
because Devlin was wearing lipstick as he looked over
the silky shoulder at Cressy and Seiver.

'Uh—Gia...' He disentangled himself and turned the
woman around.

Cressy sighed inwardly. Tall, leggy, model-slim, a sleek
knot of black hair, dark slanted eyes. No wonder Devlin
was looking slightly poleaxed by her arrival.

'Gia, this is Cressida Cross. Cressy, this is Gianetta
Alexander,' Devlin said smoothly, recovering his aplomb
as he wiped off the lipstick. 'Gia's come down from
Auckland to discuss some business with me regarding
the trust that Mark established for her before he died.
I'm her trustee...'

The sultry smile that replaced Gia's initial shock and
blatant hostility told Cressy that if she was willing to
believe that, she'd believe anything. 'Delighted to meet
you, Cressida,' she said politely, her voice as smooth as
cultured cream as she regarded Cressy's attire with dis-
taste. 'Are you one of Devlin's stable girls?'

Cressy's dislike was instant and abiding. 'Oh, no. I'm
here for pleasure, rather than business, aren't I, Devil,
darling?' she said provocatively.

Two pairs of eyes, one black, one silver, narrowed
sharply. But the silver eyes were amused as Devlin murmured, 'The pleasure of driving me mad, perhaps.' Then
he explained, 'Cressida is a famous wildlife photographer, Gia. She was stranded here by some car thieves

and graciously agreed to take some shots of Rain Lady foaling for me ...'

Cressy lifted her eyebrows. Let Gia believe *that* cunning mix of truth and fiction if she chose! There had never been anything remotely gracious in her relationship with Devlin! Then she lowered them again when she noticed the matching suitcases sitting discreetly by the hall table.

Gia followed her gaze. 'You don't mind if I stay a while, do you, Devlin?' She smiled at him with the supreme confidence of one who had never been denied the request before. 'I'll just go up to my room and unpack a few things and perhaps after lunch you can take me for a ride while we catch up on our news.' She gave a small, complacent laugh as she indicated her bags. 'I know you complain I have enough clothes here to start a salon, but I couldn't resist bringing a few new things to show you ...'

That afternoon, messing around unnecessarily in the darkroom while Gia and Devlin were 'catching up' with each other, Cressy brooded about what she had learnt during a long, uncomfortable lunch. Gia had put her point across with cunning subtlety. Every dip and turn of the conversation had revealed a depth of intimacy between the other two that made it clear that Gianetta Alexander was firmly entrenched in Devlin's life. Not only did she share part of his heritage—she also had a Spanish mother—but their ease together, the verbal shorthand with which they communicated, referring to memories, experiences, friends—a whole *history*—made Cressy's knowledge of the man she loved seem ludicrously superficial and presumptuous. And she would have had to be blind and deaf and stupid not to have drawn the obvious conclusion from Devlin's gentle response to Gia's blatant flirtatiousness and open possessiveness.

Cressy cursed as she spilled a dish of developer down the front of her jeans. She was never clumsy in the darkroom. Jealousy! It was turning her brain into mush. She was in love with the man. It was too late to pretend it didn't matter. If she was destined to suffer, why shouldn't she attempt to grab a little happiness for herself along the road to hell? Forget Max's proper priorities and go after what she wanted! Always providing, of course, that what she wanted was still on offer...

Where to start? Since Devlin had ridden off into the wide blue yonder with his simpering guest there was only one place. Seiver.

Sure enough, his dislike of the Black Widow exceeded his pleasure at keeping his own counsel and Cressy managed to extract a few pithy morsels. Devlin had looked after Gia when she went to pieces over her husband's death and the woman had made 'an infernal, fluttery nuisance' of herself ever since. She kept inviting herself to stay and invariably outstayed her welcome, but Devlin was 'too loyal' to the memory of his friend to tell her to 'buzz off'. 'She's like that creeper—jasmine—pretty to look at and smells a treat, but smothers the hell out of everything around it——'

'Oh, yes, I can see how *smothered* he feels,' said Cressy sourly, 'drooling all over her at lunch and then taking her out for a ride...they've been away for *hours*...' She could just imagine what was taking them so long. Hadn't she been on just such a ride herself?

Seiver gave her one of his contemptuous looks. 'Ya sure weren't showing any spunk at lunch. Let her wipe her feet on you, you did.'

Cressy didn't need anyone else pointing out her mistakes. 'Mind your own business,' she said fiercely, forgetting he was supposed to be an ally.

'I thought you made it mine, seeing as how you're asking my opinion—my opinion being that that woman will never let him forget how her husband died.' His voice rose to a shout as he followed her into the hall and watched her march up the stairs. 'Until he marries her! If you want him yourself, missy, you better start minding *your* business…possession is nine-tenths of the law, you know!'

There were degrees of possession, Cressy knew, as she threw herself moodily on to her bed. She surveyed her florid bedchamber. She had only just met Gia but she already knew that the woman chose to play on her weaknesses rather than her strengths, the quintessential helpless woman. She would want a man to cosset her, protect her, treat her like a piece of delicate china. She was sophisticated and extremely fastidious. She wouldn't find this room fun, as Cressy did, or appreciate its sentimental absurdity. She wouldn't see that this torrid, tasteless glory was the *real* heart and soul of Rush House, a joyful legacy of the love that had brought Devlin into the world. Gianetta Alexander was as wrong for this house as she was for the man who owned it!

Cressy got ready for dinner in a mood of simmering rebellion. She was very, very tempted to wear the lace tablecloth, but thought better of it at the last moment and reached for the repressive black dress. Devlin had said it turned him on and tonight she wanted him turned up sky-high!

She was glad when she finally swept into the drawing-room to find Gia sipping a martini in solitary splendour, wearing a screamingly expensive wine-red cocktail dress that would have made satin and lace look unbelievably tacky.

'Devlin's just taking a phone call. Sit down, Cressida. Would you like a drink?'

And give her another chance to play hostess? 'No, thanks.' Cressy sat down opposite the elegantly slanted legs.

'Have you ever done any modelling?' she asked as an innocuous opening gambit.

'Oh, goodness, no. My family wouldn't have approved at *all*,' Gia said with a charming gesture of dismay. 'And poor Mark wouldn't have liked it if I hadn't been free to travel with him. Men are so *intol-*

erant of women's careers, don't you find, Cressida? Particularly very *masculine* men, wealthy men who can afford to provide their wives with all their needs. I suppose men with a certain position to uphold feel more comfortable with the traditional kind of wife, one who's willing to make sacrifices in her own life in order to enhance his accomplishments. Fortunately for me, I never felt a driving need to assert myself in any one field. I've had a very traditional kind of female upbringing and I'm rather proud of it. I suppose that makes me seem like a very poor kind of spirit to an experienced career woman such as yourself...'

'No, of course not,' lied Cressy with murderous politeness. So Seiver was right, Gia was thinking in terms of marriage. What other unpleasant shocks did she have it in mind to deal out? 'Do you have children?'

A flicker of annoyance on the glossy features. 'My husband and I had only been married a few years when he was...killed. We hadn't even discussed children at that stage—fortunately, because I just don't think I'd have been able to cope if I'd had fatherless babies to worry about as well as all the tangles of Mark's estate. In fact, without Devlin's help I don't think I would have coped at all. He's always there when I need him——' her full lips curved in a coy expression of little-girl guilt '—which I'm afraid is rather often. But Devlin doesn't mind. If anything, we've grown so much closer since Mark's death.'

Cressy wasn't going to touch that with a barge-pole! 'It must have been very hard for you,' she murmured non-committally.

'Yes...particularly as there were all sorts of questions raised at the time, *totally* unfounded, of course, that...well...that the friendship between Devlin and myself wasn't entirely platonic, that there might have been more to the accident than just carelessness on Mark's part——'

Cressy's reaction was as taken aback as the other woman might have desired. 'You mean...*suicide*!'

'Oh, no, not suicide.' She was coolly assured. 'Mark was a good Catholic, he would never have jeopardised his immortal soul by killing himself...'

Or by agreeing to a divorce was the obvious implication. Gia wasn't talking about suicide, she was sweetly hinting at adultery and murder! For a fleeting moment Cressy seriously considered it. Devlin wasn't a man who liked to be thwarted and he still had very strong guilt feelings about his friend's death. Then she felt sick at her own gullibility. *Murder?* No. Even if the evidence had been overwhelming, Cressy wouldn't believe it. Not of Devlin. Her lack of faith in her instincts about men didn't extend that far. She knew that Devlin would never so utterly violate his personal integrity. His guilt had more complex roots. But evidently Gia expected her to believe the vile suggestion, and the knowledge was unexpectedly liberating. If this beautiful woman, with all her natural advantages, had to resort to such desperate measures it was because Devlin didn't want her. A woman who was wanted or desired by Devlin would *never* be insecure.

'As I said, the rumours were totally unfounded,' Gia continued virtuously, 'I was *never* Devlin's lover during my marriage to Mark——'

During their marriage... The qualification was a stinging slap across the face, but Cressy didn't flinch. She had guessed as much. There had to be some basis for Gianetta's possessiveness.

The woman was well into her stride now, guilelessly confiding, 'After his death, it was only natural that Devlin and I should turn to each other for support, and not surprising that our feelings should run away with us. But even though we were lovers those wretched insinuations made it necessary to be discreet about our love, at least until people forgot the slanders...'

Cressy maintained her dignity with a stiff murmur of understanding. It would not do to throw herself across the room and beat the perfidious witch to a pulp. A woman couldn't claim to love a man and at the same time deliberately grind his honour in the dust.

There was a rustle as Gia rose regally to her feet. 'I'm telling you this, Cressy, because I think it's only fair to warn you that Devlin and I share a very special relationship that has stood the test of time and great adversity,' she said kindly. 'Ah, Devlin, we were starting to wonder where you were... Drink, darling?'

'The usual, thanks.' Devlin took the chair at right angles to Cressy's, his eyes noting her abnormal paleness. 'What have you been talking about?' he asked idly.

'I was just warning Cressy that you and I go way back,' Gia said, smiling as she poured his drink from the decanter on the sideboard. 'And that she shouldn't listen to any nasty rumours about us.'

Cressy smiled faintly, her colour returning. Very clever. The perfect, unarguable truth.

'I should imagine you would be delighted to believe the most scurrilous lies about me,' said Devlin evenly as he accepted his drink, mentally cursing. He had tried to keep Gia well away from Cressy, but in his brief absence it seemed the damage had been done. He drank deeply to try to ease the angry constriction in his throat and chest. Instead the shot of whisky fed his brooding temper.

If lunch had been heavy going, dinner was even worse. To Cressy's chagrin Seiver decided to revert to obnoxious type and go back to serving her on plastic. This time, however, he went one better and gave her plastic cutlery as well. If they had been alone Cressy would have screamed like a fishwife and thrown it at him. As it was she merely gave him a vitriolic look, and when he served her main course he mumbled into her ear without moving his lips, 'Mad enough to kill yet, missy?'

She looked sideways at him and saw the evil look in the conniving eyes and was suddenly hard put to it not to laugh. 'Primed and ready,' she muttered back with a sneer to match his. 'And pointed in exactly the right direction!'

'What are you two whispering about?' growled Devlin, who had brought his third whisky to the table and then opened a bottle of red wine. No wonder Seiver was so anxious, thought Cressy as she watched him drink. Devlin's manner was that of a man who didn't give a damn about anything at this particular moment. The perfect victim for a Black Widow. There was no sign of his usual restless energy. Devlin, who was never careless, or bored, or distracted, was being all three. Even his calculated rudeness lacked its keen edge. While temper had prompted Cressy to dine off her plastic abominations with the delicacy of a born lady, Devlin had actually knocked over the water glass that Seiver had thumped pointedly in front of him ... but perhaps that had been deliberate.

'Just agreeing that you make a boorish drunkard,' said Cressy with a sugary smile.

'I'm not drunk,' he snarled, shrivelling the conspirators with an icy glare.

'No, of course not. I forgot, you're *always* this boorish....'

At first she thought he would snap at the tempting bait but instead he shrugged, and poured himself another glass of wine. He got his revenge, though, because when Gia began to gaily flirt with him, contrasting her sweet, undemanding teasing with Cressy's sour disapproval, he flirted back, with bells on.

That obviously gave the older woman the courage to broach the question that she had been bursting to ask all evening.

'I hope I'm not embarrassing you, Cressida, but is there perhaps some medical reason why you can't use porcelain plates or metal cutlery?'

Devlin swirled the wine in his glass, blatantly admiring Gia's exquisite profile as she leaned across his vision, and Cressy's steaming frustrations suddenly boiled fiercely over.

'Homicidal mania.'

Gia's mouth fell inelegantly open. 'I beg your pardon?'

'Homicidal mania. If I get anywhere near sharp objects I'm overcome by this compelling urge to kill.' Cressy snatched up Devlin's bread and butter plate, tipped the uneaten roll off it, and broke it sharply into two jagged pieces, one of which she whipped above her head, gripping it like a dagger as she leapt out of her chair, her red hair blazing around her pale face, her eyes gleaming with maniacal energy.

'Like this!' She lunged across the table.

Gia jerked back and gave a little scream. 'Devlin, do something!'

'She's only joking, Gia,' said Devlin impatiently, jolted violently out of his brooding stupor. 'Put it down, Cressy, no one finds you very funny. You cause enough breakages around here without having to resort to deliberate vandalism.'

Ah, a spark. A small spark to be sure, but at least acid impatience was better than indifference. Cressy shifted the angle of her threat towards Devlin.

'What makes you think I'm joking?' she asked throatily. She pressed the point of the jagged porcelain shard tauntingly against his snowy white shirt-front. His silver eyes flickered at the faint prick of pain. 'Maybe I've been after this all along...'

'If this is a game, Cressida, it isn't a very amusing one.' Cressy hardly heard Gia's reproachful echo of Devlin's remark; she was too busy coping with the sudden metamorphosis before her from world-weary cynicism to spitting fury. Devlin suddenly arose with such a menacing swiftness that she didn't have time to draw back, and to her horror the tip of the shard penetrated the thin silk and a miniature red blossom flowered against the

dazzling white of his breast. The piece of porcelain would
have fallen from her nerveless fingers if he hadn't surrounded them with his and held it terrifyingly steady
against the tiny pinpoint of blood.

'My heart? Is that what you're after, Cressy? You want
to slice it out of my chest and have it for bloody dessert?
Go ahead. What the hell do I need it for?'

He was mad, blackly furious. With *her*. And he had
been all evening, she realised numbly, he had just been
keeping it under control by ignoring her. Now she had
forced it out in the open. He was raw, hot and wild...all
teeth and claws, the wild panther of her nightmares.

Her brash courage deserted her. She stamped sharply
on his toe, and when he yelled hoarsely she twisted out
of his grasp and ran, screaming, past a startled Seiver
standing at the kitchen door.

'Stop him, he's gone crazy!'

She could almost feel Devlin's hot breath on the back
of her neck as she tumbled up the stairs, furious at Seiver
for just rocking on his heels, grinning with malicious
satisfaction at her predicament.

She dived into the first room she came to, which happened to be her own bedroom, and almost got the door
shut before Devlin jammed it open with his shoulder.
He knocked it shut with the same shoulder and slapped
on the light. Cressy ran around the other side of the
large bed.

'Now, calm down, Devlin——'

He gave no sign of having heard her. Planting himself
in the middle of the room, his chest heavy, his voice
rasping thickly he demanded, 'She told you that we were
lovers, didn't she?'

She was stunned. Was he furious because she knew
his secret? 'I——'

'Didn't she?'

'Yes. Yes, but——'

'She was beautiful, she was available, she needed to
touch and be touched and so did I,' he said rawly. 'What

did you expect me to do—turn my back and walk away? I'm a man, not a damned saint!'

'I realise that.' She tried to temper his raw fury, but he was having none of it. 'I——'

'It was years ago. It's done. And not even for you can I wipe out my past.'

Not even for me? Cressy moved restlessly behind the protection of the voluptuous red bed, trying to understand the source of his anger. 'I don't expect you to do that——'

'No? Then why the big performance down there?'

'I was just trying to get a reaction!' Cressy threw at him, the injustice of his sneer overcoming her confusion. 'That beautiful and available friend of yours was so busy being beautiful and available that she didn't have the wit to see that you were practically crawling into the bottle. If she makes you feel so guilty why on earth do you let her hang around? Either take her back to bed or get rid of her. Can't you see, you stupid moron, that she's using your guilt feelings to keep you on a string? She invades your home and tells lies about you and you *let* her——'

He stiffened, squaring his shoulders. 'I told you, it wasn't a lie. We had a brief affair about eight months after Mark died. I knew it was a mistake as soon as it started but I couldn't just cut her off.'

'How thoughtful of you,' Cressy was driven to grate fiercely.

'It only lasted a few weeks,' he continued doggedly. 'As far as I'm concerned she's my best friend's widow. That makes her *my* friend, always——'

'Really—is that why she hinted that some people thought that Mark's death wasn't accidental? That you might have murdered him because of a love triangle?'

'*What?*'

'That you're just waiting for the rumours to die off completely before you cleave together for ever more? If all your former lovers are so *friendly*, no wonder you need security guards!'

'And you *believe* her?' he exploded furiously. 'You actually believe I cold-bloodedly murdered my best friend in order to steal his wife!'

'No, of course I don't!' she yelled back. Why was he blaming her? It was his ex-lover who had lied, not Cressy. 'Do you think I'm an idiot? She was trying to run me off! She's probably seen off plenty of competition with that "I don't want you to be hurt by our special relationship" junk!'

'Then what the hell are we arguing about?' he demanded, his outrage dissipating.

'Because you're drunk.'

'I am not drunk!' he said bullishly.

'Good.' She unzipped her dress and he stiffened.

'What the hell are you doing now?'

'Seducing you.' She peeled off her modesty and flung it down like a gauntlet. Hands on hips, she faced him in her ubiquitous purple slip.

Devlin shook his head dumbly, transfixed by the erotic contrast of skin and hair and slippery, shiny satin.

'That's what *she's* got in mind,' Cressy told him, vibrating with outrage at the idea. 'I bet she's just waiting for you to roll back downstairs and she'll be all over you. And *you*—you'll probably let her because you feel so guilty about her. I bet you even think that it was *you* who seduced *her* into that piffling little affair.'

'It just happened,' he said tightly, knowing without looking down that his body was already betraying him. 'But she was vulnerable and I took advantage of it.' He bent to pick up her dress and held it out to her. 'I won't make the same mistake twice. Put your dress back on, Cressy, this isn't the time or the place for this. Not while Gia is still here.'

A surge of possessive fury shook her at the mention of the other woman's name. She had come this far, she wasn't going to let him back her down now or reawaken her tiresome inhibitions. She let the dress he thrust at her slide to the floor again and crossed her arms in front of her, pulling her slip over her head, her thick hair cascading back down over her bare shoulders. She was wearing the same bra and panties that he had forcibly stripped from her wet and shivering body that memorable first night. But tonight there was a subtle difference in the conformation of her body; her figure looked more lush and rounded...

'If you make a habit of taking advantage of vulnerable women why don't you make love to me? I'm vulnerable...'

'Here?' He flung out a helpless hand, knowing this was all just an erotic fantasy...

'Yes, here.' She was impatient. Perhaps he didn't think she really meant it. Perhaps he thought she would draw back at the last moment. She took his hand and backed towards the bed, pulling his strangely heavy, docile body after her. When she felt the smooth coverlet at the back of her thighs she slid her arms up around his neck and leaned into his hardness, going up on tiptoe to lay her mouth against his. It opened and accepted her, devoured her, fed her own appetite. She pulled at his jacket, dragging it down his arms. When his hands were free they came up to cup her breasts through the lacy bra, his thumbs pressing deeply into the fleshy sides, rubbing in slow, easy circles until the hardening tips showed him just where to concentrate his caresses. Tilted back against the bed she had to spread her legs for balance and he was quick to take advantage, pressing in between them, dipping so that he could align himself more satisfyingly with her need. One big, callused hand moved down the smooth column of her naked back to find the small, sensitive dimples just above the line of her panties, stroking the small indentations, finally sliding under the narrow band of elastic to cup and knead the silken curve of her buttocks. She fumbled with the buttons on his shirt, and touched the hot flesh of his chest with a small moan of delight. It wasn't enough, she was in a fever to know all of him. Her hand pushed between them to find the sleek silver clasp of his belt. Her fingertips brushed against his rigid thickness and he jerked, every muscle responding to the promise of pleasure. Then suddenly he dragged his mouth away from hers, one hand reaching down to manacle her wrist, holding her hand away from the swollen evidence of his need.

'What are you doing?' he said thickly as if awakening from a strange dream.

'Don't you know?' Cressy was halfway to heaven already in her fevered imagination.

He shook his head, like a drugged animal sluggishly responding to a goad. 'I know that this just isn't *you*——'

'You expected me to be shy?' she murmured huskily. 'But I thought Nina told you I'm not completely inexperienced...'

'This has nothing to do with experience!' Couldn't she see he was doing this for her own good? he thought raggedly. He had had too many drinks to treat her as she deserved to be treated. 'You have aggression in your character, but it's never been a sexual kind of aggression...I mean, you've never taken the initiative before——'

'I'm sorry you find it such a turn-off——' Cressy let him push her away, devastated by the realisation that he was turning her down. This sinfully sexy man really couldn't bring himself to make love to her. His body might be aroused but his mind certainly wasn't. He was acting as if she had actually *offended* him...

'That's not what I meant——'

But Cressy wasn't listening. Instead of making him lose his head, her clumsy attempt at seduction had repelled him. She was obviously ill-suited to the role of dominant, demanding wanton, and now she had irretrievably embarrassed them both. How appalled he would be if he knew what had prompted her to offer herself so flagrantly to him.

'Sorry...I guess I misunderstood,' she muttered stiffly.

'No! Yes!' He was horrified at the shame he saw in her expression as she hurriedly pulled her dress back on. He was aware that he was making a hideous mess of a vital chance. 'I was just surprised ... I don't understand why you're in such a blind rush all of a sudden. You're bound to regret it tomorrow.'

She regretted it now! 'Sorry to have embarrassed you——'

'Cressy, for God's sake, don't go. Dammit, of course I want you. But not this way. Not so *easily*——'

'Oh, I see. So I'm easy now. I apologise for coming on so strong, for being such a pushover! It'll be a cold day in hell before it'll ever happen again!'

CHAPTER NINE

'STUPID! Stupid! Stupid!'

Cressy turned off her engine and glumly stared in the rear-vision mirror at the approaching uniformed officer. A ticket was just what she needed to cap off the last, horrible few days. Actually, she corrected herself as she wound down her window, it hadn't all been horrible. Middle Island had been an interesting place and the giant tusked wetas had been just as impressive as the Conservation Department scientists had promised. Enlarged by the macro-lens, they were impressively threatening.

No, the horrible part of the four days she had spent on the island had been the discovery that her escape from Rush House had been purely physical. The challenge of capturing a newly discovered species on film had not banished Devlin from her thoughts or even relegated him to the back of her mind. Work seemed to have lost its magic healing power and she had the awful feeling that the pain of loneliness would get worse, not better, as time crept by. Even those ugly, armoured wetas had reminded her of Devlin... encased in the hard shell of his guilt, a glossy carapace which protected him from deep emotional involvement with any woman but the one to whom he was tied by the past. No wonder he had never married. Even if he didn't love Gia he couldn't bring himself to turn away from her completely because that would be like betraying his friendship with Mark all over again. In his eyes Gia was a weak and helpless victim of his mistake. He was so intelligent, so wise... and so stupid! Even more stupid than Cressy had been for running away instead of fighting for her right to love...

'Can I see your driver's licence please, madam?'

Cressy produced it, not even bothering to ask what she had done. She had probably been speeding. As usual she had been thinking about Devlin. Speed and Devlin were synonymous in her experience. Everything had happened so stunningly fast that it wasn't surprising she had made some ghastly errors of judgement. Not only had Devlin dealt fatal blows to her self-confidence and her peace of mind, he could well knock her career on the head, too, if she didn't pull herself together!

'Is this your car, Miss Cross?'

'No, it's a rental.' It had cost an arm and a leg to rent it in Hamilton to be returned in Auckland. Cressy frowned into her rear-vision mirror as she realised something. 'You're not a traffic officer!'

'No, I'm a policeman. Would you step out of the car, please, Miss Cross?'

Her mouth went dry. Now she knew why his voice had sounded oddly familiar. She was on the Thames road somewhere on the Hauraki Plains, the very road she had wandered off on her journey down. Only one policeman patrolled this beat.

'You're Constable Farradon!' she announced flatly, looking up at him. He was younger than she had imagined him to be, big and brawny, with sandy hair and a moustache.

'That's right. Could you step out of the car?' His patient implacability made her extremely wary.

'Why?'

'It's standard procedure.'

'Are you arresting me?'

'Have you done anything you think you should be arrested for?'

'No.' Falling insanely in love with a man you'd only known for a few days wasn't an indictable offence. The only cell it would qualify her for was a padded one.

He opened her door and Cressy got out reluctantly, stretching her cramped legs. She had been driving for a couple of hours, intent on getting to Auckland as quickly

as she could, following the road signs like an auto-
maton. It was getting hot. Her green sleeveless blouse
was sticking to her back and her cream cotton skirt was
crumpled. She had pulled her hair into a messy pony-
tail and hadn't bothered with make-up. She was aware
of James Farradon surveying her with faintly surprised
curiosity as he removed her keys from the ignition.

'You're not going to ask me to blow into a little bag,
are you?' she joked sourly.

'You been drinking, Miss Cross?' he drawled, without
the shadow of a smile.

'It's only eleven o'clock in the morning!'

He shrugged, as if to say there was no accounting for
people's vices. 'You didn't seem to be paying too much
attention to your driving. I've been following you for
the last few kilometres. Didn't you notice?'

Cressy looked blankly at him. Of course she hadn't
noticed him, he wasn't Devlin! 'Was I speeding?'

He shrugged again, like a parody of a laconic country
cop. 'Excuse me a minute, will you?'

He went back to his car, taking her keys with him.
The minute stretched into several and Cressy got tired
of waiting. She had five rolls of film she wanted to de-
velop. Once she had film shot, she liked to do the proofs
as soon as possible, to see if her talent had lived up to
her imagination. She stomped impatiently over to the
white police car.

'Look, are you going to——?'

There was a distant growl and Cressy looked up. The
long black ribbon of the road which stretched out in either
direction was empty, but across to their right a hazy
column of dust arose from somewhere in among the
chequer-board of green fields. The growl resolved itself
into the deep race of a powerful engine. Cressy looked
at James Farradon, sitting sideways in the front passenger seat of his car, his long legs dangling out the open
door, paperwork spread on his lap. He didn't look like
a policeman diligently carrying out his duty. He looked

like a man who was waiting for something—or someone....

Cressy's head snapped up. She narrowed her eyes against the clear morning glare, catching glimpses of the vehicle which was flashing along a farm track, one of the many unmapped private dirt roads that criss-crossed the countryside. It was a dusty red pick-up. She swore.

'Now, Miss Cross, that isn't a very ladylike thing to say, 'specially about a man who took the trouble to do so much for you.'

Now he was amused! She glared at his white grin. 'You called him, didn't you? You called him on your radio!'

'Well...I did happen to know that he would be m-ight-y interested to know you were back in the territory...'

His drawl was so absurdly exaggerated that Cressy could just picture him in some mindless American car-chase movie, playing the lawless hick cop. Which he was! He was detaining an innocent citizen for the local land-lord's pleasure.

'I could sue you for police harassment!' Cressy slapped out her hand, palm up, and demanded sharply, 'My keys, Constable.'

He clicked his tongue and put his papers aside. 'Now, where did I put those things...?' He patted his pocket. The engine roared nearer.

'Constable——'

'I just had them a moment ago.'

'You can kiss goodbye to your career if you don't hand them over *right now*!' Cressy hissed, hearing the screech of tyres turning on to the tar-sealed road several hundred metres away. Her heart raced with a mixture of terror and delight.

James Farradon stood up and nudged the car door shut with his hip, slowly unbuttoning the breast pocket in his dark blue jacket. Cressy cast a look over her shoulder. The pick-up had stopped nose-to-nose with her car. Devlin was swinging down out of the cab of the pick-up. He looked darkly furious. He began to stride towards them, his long legs slaughtering the distance, gravel from the verge scattering with each slamming impact of his boots. He was dressed in well-worn jeans and a checked shirt with the sleeves rolled up his forearms. He looked more like a hardworking cowboy than the multi-faceted tycoon he was—a hard-bitten, mean as a rattlesnake cowboy. Cressy felt more than ever that she had fallen into some ridiculous film-fantasy.

With an incoherent cry she skipped around James Farradon and scrambled into the back seat of the police car, locking the door behind her.

'OK, Constable. I surrender. I confess. Just get me out of here!' she cried.

Devlin didn't even break stride. He walked to the driver's door and wrenched it open, tossing a grim smile over at the grinning man in uniform.

'See the pick-up gets back, will you, Jamie? And her car.'

He slid in behind the wheel, started the engine and had shot away before Cressy had time to realise what was happening.

'Hey. *Hey*!' She looked out the back window at the diminishing figure of authority. James Farradon's jaw had dropped as he ate dust—his friend's dust. Serve him right for abusing his authority, thought Cressy, stricken with the hysterical urge to giggle. The thought of what the insurance company would say if she lost another rental car banished her amusement as she faced front again. 'You can't do this, you know,' she pointed out.

He didn't even bother to deny it as he spun the car on to the farm road he had just travelled moments earlier. The haze of dust that had signalled his arrival still lingered in the air.

'You're risking your friend's job. If anyone finds out what he let you do——'

The car skidded to a stop and the momentum sent Cressy spinning against the front seat and flopping violently back. Devlin swivelled round in his seat.

'Are you going to shut up?' he demanded. 'Or do you want me to gag and handcuff you?'

The savage glint in his eye told her he meant it. More than that, he would enjoy it. Satisfied with her silence, he ground the gear back into first, the car fishtailing slightly as he put his foot down.

It took him fifteen minutes of reckless driving to get back on to a farm road that she recognised, and all the way Cressy was dry-mouthed with angry trepidation. By the time he wrenched to a stop in front of the house she had managed to whip herself to a fury.

She got out of the police car on wobbly legs.

'Don't you ever, *ever* drive me that way again, you maniac!' she yelled at Devlin hoarsely.

He was already walking inside. 'Are you coming? Maybe you can call your newspaper friend and tell her what I just did. You'd probably get big bucks for the tip, not to mention another chance to sabotage my reputation and get Jamie fired into the bargain!'

'What?' Cressy stumbled after him. Loath as she was to see the Black Widow again, she knew she had no choice if she wanted to know what had caused this sizzling contempt.

She passed Seiver in the hall.

'Wouldn't like to be in your shoes,' he commented cheerfully.

Cressy followed Devlin into his office, slamming the door to express her feelings.

'Would you mind telling me what this tantrum of yours is all about? It isn't as if I took off without a word. I left you a note——'

'A note?' he snarled. '"Thanks for your hospitality"? I've had warmer communications from the tax inspector.'

'I figured that with Gia around you didn't need any extra warming.'

'Ah, yes, Gia. She's the reason that you crawled away with your tail between your legs——'

'I crawled away because of the tail between *your* legs!' Cressy yelled crudely, smouldering at the injustice. 'I always said you were a tease, Devlin Connell. You lead me on and then dump me as soon as that—that witch turns up——'

'I didn't dump you——'

'Oh, right, you were just trying to let me down lightly,' Cressy corrected jeeringly. 'Of course, you had Gia panting for you downstairs——'

'Is that why you leaked the story? Because you felt you were a woman scorned? You did it out of *pique*? My God, Cressy, whatever there was between us, I never thought you would stoop so low——'

'What story?' Cressy stopped dead in her mental tracks. Was there more at issue here than his masculine ego?

'Oh, come on, Cressy.' His laugh was short and unamused. They stared at each other for a few seconds and then he picked up the newspaper on top of the pile on his desk and threw it at her. 'How many pieces of silver were you paid for the tip-off? Quite a few, judging from the number of papers running the story.'

Cressy slowly unfolded the paper, the previous day's edition of the *Star*. It wasn't a lead story but it was fairly prominently featured on page three. The story was long on comment and short on facts; nevertheless the salient details were there: a confidential meeting of industry heads to discuss environmental issues; Devlin Connell tipped as the 'power-broker' between an influential lobby and Government caucus. The comment degenerated into speculation: was the popular and powerful Connell aiming at a political career to occupy his retirement years? Was the Government creating a 'hidden agenda' for conservation in the country?

'You think *I* did this?' asked Cressy incredulously, letting the paper fall back on to the desk.

'Not personally. I know you can't write for beans,' said Devlin, bluntly using a weapon that she had handed him in one of her trusting moments. 'But don't try and tell me this isn't just the kind of publicity your conservationist friends like to feed on——'

'I won't, because it is. But *I* certainly didn't send it to the paper.' His snort of disbelief infuriated her. 'Well, I didn't! For a start, don't you think I would have wanted to make it an exclusive, rather than lowering the value of the scoop by blabbing to all and sundry? And don't you think I would have come up with a few more juicy details instead of all these bland hints? I've got plenty of good shots of members of your "secret enclave" lurking around the grounds of Rush House, too——'

Cressy stormed closer, not noticing that, as she wound up, Devlin was unwinding, watching her spark with a greedy intensity. She jabbed him in the chest with her finger. 'But do you think I give a damn about a boring bunch of pontificating businessmen talking a lot of hot air? I don't think that they'll actually ever *do* anything. They'll just talk round and round in pompous, self-generating circles until they're back with the safe status quo. If they ever do deliver, *then* I'll bother to take some notice!'

'Cressy——' He moved impatiently under her jabbing finger but she ignored him.

'Anyone who was at the meeting could have leaked this, and you know it. It might even have been Gia for that matter, if you're dumb enough to let her have the run of your office, and you probably are. I wouldn't put anything past her. She was the one who gave me a lift to the bus when I left. Did she tell you that? Your precious *friend* couldn't wait to get me out of here.'

Cressy stopped long enough to take a much needed breath and the red haze cleared from her eyes. The expression on Devlin's face said it all. He was dancing her to his tune, damn him!

'You don't really believe I did it!' she flung at him hotly. 'You just wanted an excuse to make me squirm. Your ego needed to bounce me off some walls because I didn't stick around to watch you wallow in your incestuous guilt.'

He flinched. 'Damn you——'

'Damn *you*——'

He reached for her. The kiss was everything, and more, that she wanted. Memory didn't do him justice. He held her so tightly that she couldn't breathe, but she wouldn't have been able to anyway, the things his mouth was doing to hers. The depression of the last four days lifted, and her body fitted itself to his as if she had never been away. He pulled at the soft fabric strip binding her hair and freed its fiery mass so that he could plunge his fingers deep and hold her for his kisses. With one step, two...three, he had her backed up against the side of the filing cabinet, the smooth, hard, cold metal bracing her back contrasting with the soft, hot rigidity of his body. He pushed against her, his knee striking the grey steel cabinet as he thrust it between her thighs. He steadied himself with one hand against the metal as he splayed the other across her buttocks, lifting and adjusting her astride the hard bridge of his thigh. She clutched at him, her fingers bunching the soft check shirt, her hips jerking at the intimate friction.

He ripped his mouth from hers. 'Yes!' She barely heard his raw whisper as his stinging mouth moved down to her throat. 'That's right, move on me, honey, show me...'

The pulse at the base of her throat leapt violently against his tongue. 'Show me...' The words she had flung at him in an agony of rejection a few days ago returned to taunt her. Show him what a pushover she was? She writhed again and his hiss of satisfaction shamed her.

'No!'

This time he couldn't mistake the reason for her frantic twisting. He lifted his head. His eyes were silver slivers of desire that probed painfully under her sensitive skin. His scar seemed to throb under the taut constriction of his self-control. His hands closed on her hips, holding her still, pressing the centre of her body down on his leg. She flushed, trying to rise on tiptoe, hoping that the denim fabric of his jeans hid from him the extent of her arousal...

'Yes...' he insisted, and she felt the thick muscles of his thigh bunch and relax beneath her, a subtle goad. He knew very well what he was doing to her. She closed her eyes and pushed against his chest. God, he was so solid—hard all over...

She felt him give a strange shiver. 'I'm cold, Cressy——'

'What?' She wouldn't look.

'In my private little hell.'

He sounded so tormented that her eyes snapped open. His were very close. Her breath mingled with his. Her breasts brushed the backs of her hands as she tried to hold him away. Her mind felt filled with cotton wool, softly smothering her reason. 'W-what are you talking about?'

'It's a cold day in hell, Cressy...'

She remembered flinging that at him, too, and she hated him for gloating.

'Good. I h-hope you freeze to death!' she gritted.

'No, you don't.' He didn't seem to mind the sharp fingernails that curled into his shirt. His groan indicated that he enjoyed the small violence. He bent and nipped her breast through the cotton blouse, making a rough sound of pleasure when he discovered that she wasn't wearing a bra. Cressy struggled to cling to the wreckage of her pride.

'Gia——'

'Is gone. She left the same day you did, at my request.' His voice was steady, as inexorable as his touch.

'She was my best friend's wife, Cressy. She always will be that. But never anything more. I let her get away with certain liberties over the past few years because I felt sorry for her, and because it never mattered enough to worry me.' He abandoned her breast for the lure of her trembling mouth. 'Did you really think me such a wimp that I'd let her twist me around her spoiled little finger at the expense of something, or someone, I really care about?' he muttered against her lips. 'For all Gia's games, she doesn't really want *me*. It was always Mark for her, and in a way it still is—that's her problem. I'm only a substitute for the real thing. If Mark came back tomorrow there'd be no contest. Even if I loved her, I would never accept her love on those terms. I won't be second-best, ever, for any woman. I'm greedy enough to want to be her first choice...' He smoothed a hand over the front of Cressy's rumpled blouse, finding the damp patch over her taut nipple as his eyes looked deep into hers, plumbing her secrets. '*Your* choice, Cressy.'

She was fascinated, as always, by the swiftness with which he changed—from fury to mockery, to passion, to gentleness.

'What makes you think you'd be *my* first choice?' she asked rawly.

'If I weren't you would never have made me the generous offer of your body,' he said tensely. 'You're too conscious of your own impulsiveness to take physical commitment lightly. But you made a commitment that night...to me, and to yourself.'

A commitment? What a horribly vague word that was. She was confused, afraid to look for the meaning in his words. 'Please, let me go——' she whispered.

'I can't. Look what happened last time I tried to behave like a gentleman,' he said with gentle self-derision. 'You got straight on to your high horse and rose off into the sunset. This time what I have, I hold. The only way you're going to leave this house again, Cressy, is as my lover.'

Cressy wavered, and found her strength. Devlin didn't care enough for a lifetime, perhaps, but then how long was a lifetime? In this uncertain world it could be one night, and she would certainly have that. Two nights would be two lifetimes...

He saw the acceptance in her eyes before he felt it in the soft yielding of her body.

Devlin had swept her off her feet before, but never so totally. He picked her up and whirled her around, laughing softly.

'This is getting to be a habit,' she said huskily as he carried her up the staircase.

'I know. Exciting, isn't it?' he murmured wickedly. 'I like to hold what I have and have what I hold.'

When he got to the top of the stairs and turned towards his room, she stopped him with a soft exclamation.

'No, Devlin——'

His arms tightened in protest, lifting her higher against his chest, and she touched a finger to his scowling mouth. He thought she had changed her mind! 'Not your room, please...mine,' she pleaded throatily. To her secret amusement he looked disconcerted.

'The red room?'

'Would you mind?' she asked, slyly unbuttoning his shirt and slipping a hand inside. She felt his heart shudder. A faint flush whipped across his face. 'I think the atmosphere rather suits my mood...' she murmured provocatively, and turned her mouth so that it skimmed the crisp, dark hair that blurred the hard contours of his chest. Her tongue touched him and, looking up through her lashes, she saw that his flush was now full-blooded. His skin tasted hot and salty, spiced with his arousal.

He hustled her into the bedroom with an almost furtive haste that made her laugh. Then she wasn't laughing, but watching in awe as he tore off his shirt and his boots. She lay on the bed where he had tossed her, studying him with pride. He watched her watching him and his rough haste fell away with his discarded shirt. He unbuckled his belt and stripped it from his jeans with a slow, sensuous deliberation that sent a delicious tingling spilling through her veins. He folded the leather and placed it on the side-table and then slowly unzipped his jeans, revealing a thickening nest of hair arrowing down from his belly. Cressy stared at the tantalising V and he leant over her, the jeans parting further as he did so.

'Will you touch me the way you touched me the other night?' he asked huskily. He reached for the small hand clenched against the red coverlet and drew it to himself, pressing her fingers down into the heated nest of his lower belly. He groaned his satisfaction, his mouth covering hers as he came down on his side, hungry for more. Remembering what had happened last time she touched him, Cressy withdrew her hand and tentatively stroked his shoulders, trying to lie still as Devlin moved his mouth down her body, peeling off her blouse and skirt as he went. It was next to impossible. When he drew off her white lace panties and parted her with delicate fingers she almost fainted with the waves of pleasure that built and built until she thought she was going to explode. She wanted to bite and claw and drag him with her into the sexual wilderness and it took all her mental discipline to control her violent response. She held on so tightly to her self-control that she wasn't aware that her eyes were scrunched shut in a fierce frown or that her fists were clenched immovably at the back of his neck until Devlin broke through her concentration.

'What are you thinking about, Cressy?' he asked in a voice that sounded strangely thick and slurred.

'What?' He was lying heavily against her, the worn jeans softly abrasive against her stiff legs, his chest hair teasing at her swollen nipples. How did he expect her to think about anything at a time like this?

'You don't seem to be enjoying yourself very much. Am I doing something wrong? Something you don't like?'

She blinked up at him, half dazed with the effort of fighting her pleasure. He certainly wasn't helping, looking at her like that—his eyes hot and black, his mouth almost sultry in its sensuous fullness, glistening with moist pleasure... her pleasure.

'I'm doing my best,' she said in a tight voice, and his puzzlement deepened.

'Then why won't you touch me?'

'I *am* touching you!' Her nails dug into his neck to prove it.

'I meant more intimately. Don't you like my body? Don't you want to know the way it feels... what you can make it do for you?'

'Of course I do!' she shouted up at him. 'But you don't like women to be sexually aggressive. You don't want to be ravished——'

Devlin stiffened and Cressy went scarlet when she realised what she had blurted out in her frustration. His body began to shake and, too embarrassed to look at him, Cressy took a moment to recognise that it was with laughter. He was *laughing* at her! She struggled, hitting out at his chest, her legs thrashing as she tried to untangle them from his, almost crying at the ease with which he mastered her. It was only when he glimpsed the glitter in her eyes that he stopped laughing and began kissing her remorsefully, all over her flushed face.

'I'm sorry, I'm sorry, I wasn't laughing at you, more at me. I was beginning to think that I'd lost my t—uh, that you had some terrible hang-up. Cressy... Cressy... you little idiot, it was only that you took me by surprise the other night. Things weren't going at all the way I planned and I'd had a bit too much to drink and I was just blundering around in panic trying to make sure that you knew what you were doing. I'd love you to ravish me, truly I would. The things I want your hands and mouth to do to me are spectacularly ravishing.' His voice dropped to a velvety sexual purr. 'Please, please, darling Cressy, don't hold back. Don't hold anything back. Be as fierce and demanding as you like—I promise I'll like it too...'

'You'll have to take off those jeans first,' Cressy ordered shakily, excited by the frankly sensual invitation. He was so sexy—of course he would have no silly inhibitions...

He rolled over on to his back, and folded his arms under his head. 'Why don't you tear them off me, my little tigrillo,' he growled, the muscles of his belly taut with need. 'Consider me fair prey...'

Did he think she wouldn't dare? Cressy's breasts peaked with pleasure at the thought and Devlin had to endure an even greater torment than he had anticipated when, instead of attacking his challenge with her usual clumsy eagerness, Cressy took a leaf out of his book and ravished him with slowness, her lovely, taut breasts swaying tantalisingly close to his mouth as she teased him, brushing his belly and hips and thighs as she drew off his remaining clothes and explored his body with an innocently absorbed fascination that had him almost exploding in her hands.

When he could stand it no longer he pulled her up over him, parting her thighs so that they slid alongside his hips and pushing her upright.

'Look in the mirror, Cressy,' he invited roughly, and she lifted lustrous brown eyes and was transfixed by the shocking sight of their naked abandon, the pale feminine body with its soft curves dominating the hard, brown muscularity of the blatantly masculine one sprawled across the crimson bed.

'See how lovely you are,' Devlin praised her, his words caressing her as his hands lifted to push her tangled ginger mane back over her shoulders, fully exposing her body to her own view. He couldn't see their reflection but he could see her response to it and he found it intensely arousing. He clenched his teeth in sweet agony at the swelling, pulsing hardness in his groin. He had deliberately drawn her attention to the mirror because he hadn't wanted her to get the kind of unpleasant shock that had turned him off when he had inadvertently caught sight of himself in the grip of sexual frenzy. Once again it seemed that he had underestimated his innocent seductress. Her sensuality burnt as brightly as the soft growth that nestled between her creamy thighs. Soon he would be nestled there, too. She was a lover's delight...voluptuous and warm and exciting, sweetly enticing in her innocent abandonment to each new pleasure he introduced...

Her lips parted as his hands drifted down to cup her lush breasts, framing them with his fingers to emphasise their fullness. His hands on her body made an incredibly erotic picture and Cressy couldn't tear her eyes away as he stroked her, describing the pleasure he got from looking at her and touching her, drawing her attention to the reaction of his own body as she watched him in the mirror.

'We look so right together, don't we? We fit so well.' He undulated his hips so that she felt him, thick with desire, press against the open heart of her. 'I want you to make love to me like this one day...mistress of all you survey, proudly astride your kingdom. Never feel afraid or ashamed of the sexuality between us, Cressy, because it's a rare and beautiful thing...' His back arched as she moved on him experimentally. His hands gripped her waist and he rolled over, quickly pinning himself between her thighs as he captured her sigh of wicked disappointment with his tongue, thrusting it back inside her mouth.

'But for now I need to be the master...for all your splendid fierceness you're small and I'm large, I'm experienced and you're not...very. I think it will be better for you this way, this time...'

Better? The man was definitely a master—of understatement as well as lovemaking, thought Cressy muzzily, somewhere deep within the dark reaches of the night that followed. If there was a better way to make love then she doubted she would be able to survive it! Curled against his sated, sleeping body she felt as exhilarated and exhausted as if she had run a race. Perhaps she had. Didn't they say that sex was the best natural exercise? With Devlin as a lover she would be the fittest woman on earth!

Even though he hadn't said that he loved her, he made her *feel* loved. He had been tender, cherishing, as well as wild and passionate, taking care to protect her even though it had meant an interruption to the rhythm of their lovemaking and, that first time, a visit to his room. He had teased her about it, made her laugh, and been insufferably proud of himself when he had made her cry, too... tears of weak pleasure that he had drunk like wine from her eyes.

Oh, he was a man all right, her Devlin. She curled herself even closer, pushing a tender thigh between his. *Her* Devlin. He was that, though he might not be willing to admit it yet. Give her time, and she would make him... time to tempt the Devil with the sweet apple of love...

CHAPTER TEN

WAKING up in bed with the man she loved was another new experience that Cressy had been looking forward to. She certainly hadn't expected to be shaken awake to find *two* men in her bedroom, and the ghastly spectre of a third!

'He says he's *who*?' whispered Cressy blearily.

'Your father. He wants to speak to you. *Now*.' Seiver grinned smugly at her horror and Cressy slid a look at Devlin out of the corner of her eye. He was sprawled on his stomach beside her, unmoving except for the slow flex of his naked shoulders as he breathed. Gorgeous...

'He's not gonna wake up 'less you prod him. He's a deep sleeper,' commented Seiver blandly, and Cressy jerked her eyes away from the unconscious man, struggling to concentrate. Her *father*? What did he want, and how had he known where to find her?

'You gonna come and take this call or do I tell your Dad that you're otherwise occupied?' said Seiver slyly while she dithered.

She glared at him. 'Yes, I'll take the call, you grubby old man, if you'll take your carcass out of here so I can get up!' Seiver snorted and spun on his heel and Cressy suddenly thought it might be inadvisable to provoke him. 'I'll take it in the master bedroom. Don't you say anything to him!'

He turned to raise falsely innocent eyebrows. 'What is there to say? None of my business who you choose to sleep with without the benefit of matrimony,' he said virtuously.

'No, it isn't!' Cressy hissed, blushing furiously as he chuckled.

'Devlin, now—he's a different matter. Don't like to
see a good man led astray by loose women. You ain't
just toying with him, are you, missy? You are gonna
make an honest man of him...?'

Trust Seiver to turn his blessing into an insult! Cressy
would have thrown her pillow at him but he was too
quick for her. 'Your father's on line two,' he said from
out in the hall. 'And you'd better be quick. He sounds
like a man in a hurry!'

Cressy slid out of bed and reluctantly into the rumpled
skirt and blouse which was all she had to wear. She was
always losing her wardrobe around Devlin! As she moved
towards the door Devlin stirred and rolled over, taking
the red satin sheets with him, but he showed no sign of
consciousness and Cressy paused to admire him. His impressive chest and outflung arms were lax in sleep, the
suppleness concealing the fluid outlines of muscle that
powered his body. It amazed her that a man so strong
and hard could be so gentle. The first time he had entered her he had hurt her a little in spite of his careful
preparation, and she had seen her pain mirrored in his
face. It was a long time since she had welcomed a man
inside her body, and Devlin acknowledged the gift
gracefully, moving only very slowly, holding her eyes with
his so that he could read and interpret her every need
as she re-learned the rhythms of life. He hadn't hurt her
again, even later, when he had lost his head and driven
relentlessly for his own satisfaction. It had been a heady
sensation to feel him shuddering helplessly in her arms,
crying out hoarsely in Spanish. She only wished she had
understood what he was saying! He had loved her lavishly well and she had ached with the desire to tell him
how much his loving meant to her. She would, too, after
she had got rid of Max...

'Where are you? Still in Turkey? This is a *terrible*
line——'

'Typical Telecom...just got in!' Cressy held the
crackling receiver away from her ear. Max always shouted

on the phone, probably because he was so used to having to talk over background gunfire. Slowly what he was trying to tell her registered.

'You're in *Auckland*! Where? Are you at the flat?'

'Early flight...congratulations...'

Cressy now had the receiver glued to her ear. Had Max received another award? Had Nina told him where to ring? But even Nina hadn't known she would be here. Cressy had accepted Gianetta's offer of a lift to the nearest main road because it had seemed like the only way to get away from Rush House without alerting Devlin. Instead of dumping her at the roadside, as she had half expected Gia to, the woman had actually waited until Cressy flagged down a bus and had even given her the fare to speed her on her way. By the time she had got to Hamilton police station Cressy had been so desperate for a shoulder to cry on that she had rung Nina and let it all hang out. Maybe her friend had told Max to ring Middle Island and, finding that she had gone, shrewdly guessed that the 'two-timing monster' might prove to have some redeeming features after all!

'...look forward...seeing...Rush House——'

'What?' Cressy realised in horror what he was intending to do. 'Max, no, you can't come down here!'

'Have to see...happening...little girl...'

'No—Max——!' What had Nina told him? In spite of his cavalier attitude to his own life and the fact that he had taught her early to be completely independent, every now and then her father succumbed to a fit of belated paternal conscience and decided to meddle. Cressy blanched at the thought of Max meeting Devlin head-on. If Max thought his only child wasn't being treated to the respect she deserved he was quite capable of throwing a few punches to make his point. Or, worse, if he discovered that Cressy was at last genuinely in love with a man who was actually worthy of her he might take it into his stubborn head to act the heavy father!

'Look, Dad, you stay right there with Nina, I'll come to you,' she said urgently, starting to panic.

'Assignment . . . can't waste time . . .'

'*No!* Look——' she glanced at the slim digital clock on Devlin's bedroom desk '——I can be with you in a couple of hours. That's all, Dad, a couple of hours——' Devlin would have to lend her a car if James Farradon hadn't delivered her rental yet. He, of all people, would understand the demands of family duty . . . 'Promise me you'll stay there. *Promise*?'

His reply was totally garbled by the rhythmic thundering of the static and Cressy's panic was complete. Finally, the only thing she could do was hang up and redial the flat, but all she got was an engaged signal. She waited as long as she dared before she reasoned that Max must be still there, making a few more calls. It wasn't even seven a.m. yet. If he hadn't had breakfast it was a while before he would leave—breakfast was the one meal he never, *never* hurried, bullets or no bullets.

Cressy rushed back to her room and stared in shock at the empty bed. Did I dream him, my demon lover? she wondered light-headedly. Did he wake up disappointed because I wasn't there? Or grateful that there would be no morning-after awkwardness?

She gave her face and hair a lick and a promise and she scurried downstairs to the kitchen.

'Where is he?' she demanded of Seiver, who was drinking coffee and reading the morning paper.

'Who?'

Cressy snatched his paper out of his hand. 'Devlin!'

He snatched the paper back. 'The vet called on the other line. The stud along the road has got a mare down and it could be something infectious. She was up here being serviced a week ago by Rome Legend, so Devlin and John have gone to take a look.'

Cressy was almost dancing in frustration. 'But I have to see him. Can you take me there?' She couldn't let him think she was running away again. He might give up chasing her!

'Nope. If it is infectious they'll have to put the place into quarantine. He said for me to be sure and tell you he'd be back as quick as he could.'

'But I really can't wait! I have to go to Auckland to see my father. I *have* to. Oh, God, what am I going to *do*?' Visions of panic danced in her head. If Devlin was planning to take up a political career shortly, the last thing he needed was to get on the wrong side of Max. Max had shouted down heads of state and terrorists. Max loved to publicly roast people for their wrongdoings. The mistress of a politician must be discreet above all else and her father was indiscretion personified. If she could just talk to Max first, explain the delicate state of her relationship with Devlin, she could smooth the way to a properly choreographed meeting between the two men she loved most in the world.

'I'll just have to write Devlin a note and you can give it to him,' she decided frantically. A very different note from last time. 'He wouldn't mind if I borrowed one of his cars, would he? Only for a few hours. I'd be back this afternoon——'

'What's the matter with yours? Farradon brought it back last night. Your stuff is in the hall——'

'Oh, great!' She felt an enormous rush of relief that something was going right.

It wasn't quite that easy, of course. How did you trust your future to a piece of paper? It took her four attempts and a precious fifteen minutes to get a note that was informative without being too revealing, pleading without being begging, and warmly affectionate without being overly presumptuous. Love wasn't mentioned but it was strongly implied...

She stuffed the letter into Seiver's hand with a threat that if he didn't pass it on she would come back and make him eat her words. He didn't respond to her flippancy, saying only, gruffly, 'As long as you do come back, missy...'

In the hall she hesitated. If she was going back to the flat she might as well take back the equipment she wouldn't need, and she'd take her suitcase, too, so that she could swap her practical jeans and T-shirts for some of the pretty, feminine clothes she possessed. She couldn't afford to be complacent, not with a man like Devlin.

She was lugging everything across the hall when a tall, dark and rather beautiful older woman stepped across the threshold. Her ink-black hair was streaked with iron-grey but it only made her aristocratic features look even more distinguished. She was dressed in a gorgeous apricot silk suit that flattered her upright carriage.

'I am Mariana Connell,' she announced. 'Where is my son?' The Spanish accent barely inflected the perfect speech.

Cressy's suitcase slipped from her suddenly sweaty palm and she blushed all over, certain Devlin's mother would be horrified to know that this crumpled-looking female with scarcely brushed ginger hair had just climbed out of his—her—*their*—bed of sin.

'I...I...he's gone out,' she croaked.

'Really? How rude of him.' Mariana advanced like a beautiful bird of prey swooping on a helpless sparrow. 'And you, are you leaving also?' Her tone was that of a polite enquiry but Cressy saw the deep disapproval in the black eyes, and her pride flinched as Señora Connell went on, 'But I, also, am being rude, not allowing you to introduce yourself...?' Her eyebrows rose, inviting Cressy to rectify the omission. She's only *minor* aristocracy, Cressy told herself stoutly, and she married a commoner...

She lifted her chin and opened her mouth but her name stuck in her throat as she suddenly noticed the other woman. Just as tall and dark and aristocratic, but younger, a slender, sloe-eyed Spanish beauty, equally beautifully dressed. She smiled sweetly at Cressy, the quintessential pliant and protected Spanish maiden.

'Ana, come and meet Devlin's friend.' Mariana Connell held out her hand fondly to the beautiful girl. 'Ana Sebastian is also a friend of Devlin's and a very much loved member of the family. In fact, she and Devlin were engaged at one time, a few years ago...'

Ana blushed, as if her companion had said something indecent, and to Cressy's mind she had. *This* was Nina's sultry *señorita*? She looked barely out of her teens—she must have been a *baby* when he had put a ring on her finger. Had Devlin decided that she was too young for him? Now that she was older, had he decided to fulfil his earlier promise? Was she here at Devlin's invitation—or his mother's? Did Devlin know *any* women, besides Cressy, who weren't utterly gorgeous?

'I really must go, if you'll excuse me,' said Cressy, forgetting the suitcase that had slipped out of her hand. The first step she took sent her tumbling to her knees.

Ana knelt gracefully to help her, making Cressy hate her all the more for being so nice. When she stumbled to her feet again, gripping her case, she found Devlin's mother regarding her with an amused glint in the dark eyes, her full red mouth curved in what Cressy interpreted as a sneer.

'Where the hell do you think you're going?'

The three of them whirled around and Cressy's heart gave a thump. Devlin was back. Like her he was wearing yesterday's clothes, and he was unshaven, the shadow on his chin blue-black. There were weary lines on his face that Cressy had never noticed before. His olive skin looked pale and his scar stood out prominently. He ignored his mother's delighted greeting and Ana's blush and strode over to Cressy.

'I said, where the *hell*——?'

'I heard what you said!' said Cressy stiffly. She didn't want to give his mother a worse impression than the one she already had by screaming at her son like a fishwife.

Through the front door someone else came shuffling, a squat little man in a dark suit and cap heaving two enormous suitcases, his mouth moving in soundless curses as he struggled with the heavy bags. The chauffeur, guessed Cressy, seeing the highly polished black Rolls-Royce drawn up at the bottom of the steps.

'Well?' Devlin looked at her, festooned with gear, and snatched her suitcase out of her hand, setting it down out of reach. 'What's your excuse this time?'

'I need to go back to Auckland——'

'I see,' he said icily, every bit as imperious as his mother. 'You need. *You* need! Have you ever bothered to ask yourself what *I* need, Cressy? Am I so utterly unimportant to you?' His voice thickened. 'I've been out there worrying that I may have to have my whole stable put down and all you can think about is your-self——'

'Devlin——' His mother's tentative interruption was ignored by the two combatants.

'What did the vet say?' asked Cressy, suddenly appalled at her thoughtlessness. Was that why he was looking so haggard? 'Is it something infectious——?'

'As it happens, no, but what do you care? All I am to you is a damned convenience. I'm good enough for you in bed, but not enough to merit any consideration out of it. It's not as if I've ever threatened your work, dammit! Quite the reverse. Do you *know* how I feel being relegated to a one-night stand? I'll tell you: I feel like an animal. Like Rome Legend—performing on command when a mare's in heat, but not expected to distinguish one from another. Is that the way you think of me?'

By this time Cressy's face was as red as her hair. How could he? How *could* he say that in front of his snooty mother? Let him find her note later, and come to her and grovel. If she had to go, at least she could go in dignity!

No, to hell with dignity, she would go in style!

She turned, and flicked a wrist towards the chauffeur. 'You! Carry my bag out to my car—the Honda.'

There was a split second of dead silence and then the little man tugged his cap.

'Yes, ma'am,' he said smartly, and gave her a friendly grin as he swept up her case. That gave her the courage to add haughtily, 'And you may as well take these as well,' handing over a couple of camera bags. He winked at her and trotted out the door.

When she faced the other three it was to find that they were still frozen in varying attitudes of shock.

'Goodbye, Devlin,' she said, in an acid little voice that thawed his stiff expression. 'Goodbye, Señora Connell, Señorita Sebastian.'

She swept out the door. It had hurt to see Mariana Connell and her son recover to exchange a look of such unreadable blandness that Cressy just *knew* they were killing themselves with laughter inside at her ridiculous presumption...

The chauffeur put her cases in the boot and opened the car door for her without even being asked. He said something to her as she got in but Cressy was both blind and deaf to everything but the thundering fear and rage inside.

She reversed to straighten the car and saw Devlin leap down the front steps in a single bound, his mother following more sedately, laughing. Devlin was grinning, too, and Cressy rammed her foot down hard on the accelerator, only realising that she had forgotten to change gear as the car lurched violently backwards. She felt a vibrating thump, and heard an ominous crash and tinkle. She turned the ignition off and sat for a moment with her eyes closed, putting off the moment when she would have to face fresh humiliation. The car door opened.

'Are you all right, Cressida?'

She nodded, and dazedly let the chauffeur help her out of her car. She walked unsteadily round to the back to look at the damage. The back of her Honda was

crumpled like a can. The front driver's door of the
Rolls-Royce had withstood the blow with due fortitude,
but there was still a very definite dent in the gleaming
panel. She bit her lip, not daring to look at Devlin, who
had crunched up beside her.

'You've really done it now, Crash,' he commented
brutally.

Cressy clenched her fists at the horrid nickname, but,
before she could force out the necessarily abject apol-
ogies, Mariana Connell said, 'It was hardly Cressida's
fault, Devlin. Heavens, didn't we teach you better
manners? You storm in and start throwing your weight
around like a bad-tempered schoolboy—and a rude one
at that—no wonder Cressida was too upset to concentrate on her driving. I think you should apologise for
your grossly offensive remarks right now, Devlin. And
I certainly think you should offer to pay for the damage!'

'Typical woman. Try and get a man to take the blame!'

Cressy was startled by the chauffeur's outburst, but
Devlin's mother didn't turn a hair at this rank
insubordination.

'Typical of a man to put all the blame on a woman,'
she countered swiftly. 'Look how you parked this thing,
all crooked. You should take partial responsibility, too,
Joshua Connell. If it weren't for you we would have had
a nice, inexpensive car to repair, but you couldn't just
rent a Rolls for a few weeks—no, you had to *buy* one.
Well, it serves you for being ridiculously extravagant!'

Joshua *Connell*? Cressy forgot the lesser horror in the
greater one. She looked from the squat little man to the
beautiful woman, to the face of the man beside her.

He nodded gravely. 'My father,' he said, quite kindly
in the circumstances.

'Oh, no!' Cressy's humiliation was complete. And she
had treated him like a servant!

'Don't worry, Cressida. People often don't realise
we're married,' said Mariana Connell consolingly,
putting her arm around Cressy's stiff shoulders. 'I should

warn you that the Connell men are very deceptive in
their looks. I mean, you'd never know, looking down
at Joshua, that he has this inexplicable, and I might add
thoroughly tiresome, fascination for women!' Her
husband grinned and Cressy could suddenly see the attraction of that jaunty toughness, the bone-deep confidence in his masculinity that his son shared.

'And looking at that rather intelligent head on my
son's handsome shoulders,' Mariana continued, 'you'd
never imagine that he has a brain the size and capacity
of a monkey's. Or so it would seem from his behaviour.
He hasn't even given you a ring, I see, so he can hardly
expect to be treated with the consideration of a proper
fiancé.' She tilted her head, surveying her son with the
same kind of amusement that she had directed at Cressy
earlier. 'You know, there *is* a certain similarity between
Devlin and one of his stallions. He has that same irritating air of sleek complacency. My advice, Cressida, is
to carry on the way you are. He obviously needs the
workout!'

'Do you mind, Mother? Cressy is skittish enough as
it is.' Devlin removed his mother's arm and replaced it
with his own as Cressy began to recover the wits that
had deserted her when his mother had mentioned a ring.

'But...I...Devlin and I...we're not...I mean we're
only lovers——' She stopped, a hand over her clumsy
mouth, aghast at what she had said, her wide eyes flying
to Ana's face. The girl smiled gently, and Cressy felt
awful. What was even more awful was her mean sense
of triumph. As far as Cressy knew, Devlin hadn't even
bothered to glance at his sultry *señorita*. Hardly the actions of a man in the throes of requited love!

'Devlin!' His father's bark suddenly had all the authority that his stature lacked. 'I thought you said you
were marrying the girl? We didn't come all this way just
to watch her slip through your fingers, you know.'

'Dad——'

'You—you told them that we were getting *married*?' Cressy's voice was an appalled squeak.

Devlin smiled uneasily.

'He rang us, a couple of days ago, to prepare us,' his mother said. 'To ask us to come and meet you——'

A couple of days? Cressy touched her hand to her forehead. She felt dizzy. She must have concussion. A couple of days ago she and Devlin had been in separate universes.

'Are you all right? Did you hit your head, Cressida? Stop crowding her, Devlin, give the girl some air.' Joshua Connell lifted her out of his son's grasp with astonishing strength and sat her on the warm bonnet of the injured Rolls.

'Cressy? Did you hit your head?' Devlin brushed back her vivid hair so he could study her unblemished forehead in the sharp morning sunlight. 'Darling, are you hurt?'

'Perhaps you'd like some tea,' said Ana kindly. 'Why don't I go and ask Seiver to make some? And I want to ring my husband in Wellington. He'll be so surprised to hear I'm only a few hundred kilometres away.'

'Don't worry, Cressida, everything will be all right,' said Mariana, elbowing her way past the two men to pat Cressy's hand.

'Ana's already married?' Cressy was trying to sort the shocks into comprehensible order.

'Mmm. To someone far more suitable for her than Devlin,' his mother said with fond contempt. 'I see now that we must have given you a bad fright turning up like this out of nowhere. Goodness knows what you thought when I introduced Ana the way I did! She's been married to my nephew, who travels promoting the family wine interests, for the last two years. She came with us because she has marvellous news for Diego that she wanted to deliver in person. She's pregnant. So, my sister is to have a grandchild before I . . . unless you two . . . ?'

She managed to look faintly disapproving and wickedly hopeful all at once.

'Give us a chance, Mother,' said Devlin mildly, and suddenly the full extent of his monumental arrogance finally sank through. Cressy began to shake with love and fury.

She wrestled herself free of the Connells' concern and slid off the bonnet, straightening her clothing and taking a deep, steadying breath.

'I——'

The faint beating that had provided a subtle counter-point to the conversation suddenly began a swirling fury. Cressy had to push her skirt down with her hands as it whipped up around her thighs. Her hair blew across her eyes, blinding her as the roar thundered in her ears and tiny pieces of the gravel driveway spat sharply at her ankles. When the whirlwind died to a slow chop-chop she dragged the hair out of her eyes to see the helicopter which had landed on the flat grassed area beside the house. A man was climbing out, bending low, yelling something to the pilot.

Hands still anchoring the creased skirt against her thighs, Cressy watched in disbelief as the man turned and began moving towards them with a familiar lope. Even more familiar was the huge scratched black camera case festooned with airline stickers that was slung over his shoulder.

'Oh, no...' Now she knew why the line to Max had been so bad. He hadn't been ringing from Auckland, but from a helicopter in mid-flight. 'Oh, *no*!'

'I thought you'd be pleased to see your father,' Devlin murmured, unnerved by her reaction.

Not just any old helicopter, Cressy realised. Devlin's! 'You arranged this?' she croaked.

'That's not quite the word I'd use in connection with your father,' he replied carefully. 'I get the feeling that the only arrangements he's happy with are his own. I got Frank to find out where he was through one of the

Press agencies and, since he wasn't accessible by phone, I sent him a telex via the local Press Association bureau. The next thing I know he's in Auckland, demanding to see me. I had to go to him.'

'You've already met Max?'

'A couple of days ago. He had a few contacts to look up before he followed me back down——'

'You—and Max?' Together? Alone? Cressy had been afraid of an ugly confrontation between the two men, but she realised there were worse things—like Devlin and Max deciding her future for her, like ruthlessly benevolent dictators.

'Cress! Surprised?' She was enveloped in a bear-hug punctuated by exclamations that confirmed her worst fears. 'I know I was! Thought it was a joke at first! My girl? You know I was always terrified you might marry one of those wimps you could trot around on a leash. Or fall for a moron who'd want you to stay home and do weddings and fashion spreads. This guy has his head screwed on. Talking to him is like—well, like talking to myself!'

Max beamed at her, having dished out his highest compliment, his pleasure undimmed by the fact that his daughter was standing like a statue in his arms.

'And you must be Devlin's parents. Pleased to meet you!' He shook hands vigorously with Mariana as she introduced herself and clapped Joshua soundly on the back. 'Great son you have there. Knows what he wants and goes for it ... Say, has someone had an accident?' He whistled as he noticed the dented Rolls. 'It wasn't Cressy, was it?'

'Yes, as it happens it was,' gritted Cressy when she could get a word in edgeways. 'And there's going to be another if someone doesn't explain what's going on!'

'What's going on is that my daughter doesn't marry a man without me being there to give her away!' her father stated. 'I had to dump some great stories for this, and I can't stay longer than a few days, so let's get on

with it. Of course, being in a rush doesn't mean to say
we can't do it in style. Who's doing the organisation?
I'll be taking the wedding photos, of course, but I never
was much good at social etiquette. You can show me all
that stuff, Mariana, you look like a woman with plenty
of style. Since I'll be paying for it, naturally I should
have the last word, but I'm not a man who can't take
advice gracefully——'

'Now just a minute. There isn't going to be any
wedding!' Cressy exploded, cutting off that last, outrageous lie of her father's.

'Cressy——'

She ignored the warning in Devlin's voice. He had no
right to do this to her. 'For the simple reason that Devlin
has never asked me to marry him,' she finished coldly.
'This is the first I've heard any suggestion of a per-
manent arrangement. As far as I'm concerned all I ever
was to Devlin was a quick roll in the hay.' She ignored
the gasps and went grimly on. 'And besides, I would
never be such an idiot as to marry a man I don't know,
let alone an arrogant dictator.' She glared at her father.
'If he's so great, Max, *you* marry him. You certainly
seem to know more about his plans than I do. I always
thought that a marriage should be built on love and trust,
and communication, and as far as I'm concerned Devlin
isn't even in the running! Next time you're planning a
surprise, Devlin, try making sure it's a *welcome* one!'

'Devlin, is this true? You haven't told her how you
feel? You've sprung this all on her without asking
first...?' His mother sounded horrified. At least someone
was on her side, thought Cressy wistfully. 'Cressy, when
he called us in Seville he told us he loved you, and that
we would too. He said you liked my ghastly red room
and I just *knew* you must be the right one. Oh, *Devlin*!'
She spilled into short, sharp Spanish.

'Been pretty stupid, haven't you, son?' said his father.

'I thought you said you knew what you were doing!'
Cressy's father demanded.

'Yes, well, I...there wasn't time...' Devlin turned his back on the parental criticism. 'I wasn't being arrogant, Cressy.' Her eyes widened in disbelief and he amended with a sullen desperation, 'Yes, well...only a little...I just wanted, needed, to talk out my feelings...to talk *about* you, since I couldn't talk *with* you, because you'd run off——!' He broke off the rising accusation hurriedly, rubbing his scar with a finger that Cressy was fascinated to notice was trembling. 'I just wanted to prepare them...I only said I *wanted* to marry you—well, OK, maybe I did use the word "intend", but only because I didn't want to contemplate the alternative... God, Cressy, I certainly didn't expect all of them—or any of them—to descend on us this quickly!'

'What were you going to allow me, another day or two to get used to you?' demanded Cressy sarcastically.

'No, actually, a lifetime...'

Cressy's breath caught in her throat as he took her clenched hands into his and drew them to his chest. He was as grave as she had ever seen him, ignoring everything but her. 'I've made an utter mess of this, but please don't hold it against me. Falling in love at my age is a terrifying experience. *You* terrify me. You have such power over me that I can't accept that I have none over you. I told you last night how I felt but maybe I wasn't very coherent—perhaps I didn't even say it in English. If I tell you now that I love you and want to marry you, will you say yes, Cressy?'

Was he saying these things because of their audience? Because it was expected of him? Because he needed the respectability of a wife for his political career? Cressy shook her head, trying to clear it of the wonderful terror of knowing that his reasons didn't matter. She would have him...

He coolly sliced through her momentary silence. 'OK, if you won't marry me because you don't think we've had enough time together, then why don't we just live together for a while? *Then* we can get married—providing, of course, that the romantic bloom hasn't worn off in the meantime. Is that what you want, Cressy? A trial marriage? To be a live-in lover rather than a wife?' His tone was cynical, ironic, and coldly calculating— and caused a muted uproar around them.

'Now just a damned minute——!' Max was rapidly coming to the conclusion that Devlin was not such a great guy after all.

'Devlin, you can't talk about it out here——' Mariana sounded more puzzled than upset.

'Thought you had better taste, boy,' his father snapped.

Only Cressy perceived the turbulent truth behind the cool challenge. He knew she loved him, but he wanted only what she was prepared to give freely.

'What about your political masters—won't they object to a candidate who didn't project the right cosy family image?'

He knew immediately what was in her mind. 'Politics as such doesn't interest me. And even if it did, it would be on my own terms.'

'The only terms you recognise. No wonder you and Max got on,' Cressy sighed, delight shimmering through her body.

'Well, Cressy? Would you rather be my mistress than my wife?' he demanded, his humbleness not quite overriding his grim determination.

Cressy spread her fingers over his warm chest and smiled at him, a prim tucking of her small mouth that made him want to carry her off and make love to her until that little satiny pink bow unravelled and curled around him, moist and silky-sweet.

Her answer slid into his erotic dream, shattering it. 'Yes.'

'What?'

'Yes, I'd like to be your mistress...'

It was worth it just to see his face. The colour came and went as if she had actually struck him. He hadn't been prepared for rejection, not really. Cressy enjoyed her victory while she could; she knew it wouldn't last long. Soon he would begin to think.

Sure enough, while Max spluttered his chagrin and Mariana put her slender hands to her flushed face and Joshua harrumphed in embarrassment, Devlin's expression underwent a rapid change. His shock became admiration, amusement... delight. He laughed, offending everyone anew—except Cressy.

Then he sobered and Cressy knew herself rich beyond imagining as he said gently, 'You do me great honour.'

'What do you mean, honour?' his father snorted. 'She just told you she doesn't want to marry you!'

'Is that what you said, Cressy?' Devlin murmured, moving closer, tempted by the love spicing her cinnamon eyes. 'Funny, I thought I just heard you say that you loved me enough to be anything I desired...'

'Not in a language *I* understand!' growled Max.

Cressy smiled. How absurd to think that she and Devlin didn't know each other. When it really mattered they communicated perfectly.

'I do,' she said.

'Now you tell me,' he said wryly. 'Did you have to put me through hell first?'

'I had to give the Devil his due.' She linked her arms around his neck. 'He deserved it, all that arrogance and pride. That's why he got tipped out of heaven in the first place!'

'And now paradise is regained,' he murmured against her mouth, tasting victory in his own turn. Still kissing her, he picked her up. 'Mustn't break with tradition,' he purred, and began to carry her back towards the house.

As they went through the doors and Devlin shouted to Seiver for champagne, Cressy heard her aggrieved father's voice rising behind them on the effervescent spring air.

'Well? Is there going to be any damned marriage or not...? Is that some weird Spanish tradition—carrying the bride across the threshold *before* the wedding? Will someone tell me what's going on? Why are you two smiling...?'

Oh, there would be a marriage all right, thought Cressy dreamily, but it wouldn't be damned. They had speed, training and endurance on their side. Why, their love had already survived hostility, suspicion, threats, misunderstandings, arguments, kidnapping, abandonment...more trials than most relationships faced in a whole lifetime!

JAYNE ANN KRENTZ

A two-part epic tale from one of today's most popular romance novelists!

Dreams
Parts One & Two

The warrior died at her feet, his blood running out of the cave entrance and mingling with the waterfall. With his last breath he cursed the woman— told her that her spirit would remain chained in the cave forever until a child was created and born there....

So goes the ancient legend of the Chained Lady and the curse that bound her throughout the ages—until destiny brought Diana Prentice and Colby Savager together under the influence of forces beyond their understanding. Suddenly they were both haunted by dreams that linked past and present, while their waking hours were filled with danger. Only when Colby, Diana's modern-day warrior, learned to love, could those dark forces be vanquished. Only then could Diana set the Chained Lady free....

HARLEQUIN
Romance®

**HARLEQUIN ROMANCE
IS BETTING ON LOVE!**

And The Bridal Collection's
September title is a sure bet.

**JACK OF HEARTS (#3218)
by Heather Allison**

THE BRIDAL COLLECTION

THE BRIDE played her part.
THE GROOM played for keeps.
THEIR WEDDING was in the cards!

Available in August in
THE BRIDAL COLLECTION:

**THE BEST-MADE PLANS (#3214)
by Leigh Michaels**

Harlequin Romance

Wherever Harlequin
books are sold.

WELCOME TO

The quintessential small town, where everyone knows everybody else!

Finally, books that capture the pleasure of tuning in to your favorite TV show!

GREAT READING...GREAT SAVINGS...AND A FABULOUS FREE GIFT!

Each book set in Tyler is a self-contained love story; together, the twelve novels stitch the fabric of the community. The covers honor the old American tradition of quilting; each cover depicts a patch of the large Tyler quilt.

With Tyler you can receive a fabulous gift, ABSOLUTELY FREE, by collecting proofs-of-purchase found in each Tyler book. And use our special Tyler coupons to save on your next TYLER book purchase.

Join your friends at Tyler for the seventh book, ARROWPOINT by Suzanne Ellison, available in September.

Rumors fly about the death at the old lodge! What happens when Renata Meyer finds an ancient Indian sitting cross-legged on her lawn?

Back by Popular Demand

Janet Dailey

Americana

Janet Dailey takes you on a romantic tour of America through fifty favorite Harlequin Presents novels, each one set in a different state and researched by Janet and her husband, Bill.

A journey of a lifetime. The perfect collectible series!

September titles
#39 RHODE ISLAND
Strange Bedfellow
#40 SOUTH CAROLINA
Low Country Liar

Fall in love with

Harlequin Superromance®

Passionate.
Love that strikes like lightning. Drama that will touch your heart.

Provocative.
As new and exciting as today's headlines.

Poignant.
Stories of men and women like you. People who affirm the values of loving, caring and commitment in today's complex world.

At 300 pages, Superromance novels will give you even more hours of enjoyment.

Look for four new titles every month.

Harlequin Superromance
"Books that will make you laugh and cry."

HARLEQUIN
American Romance®

American Romance's year-long celebration continues.... Join your favorite authors as they celebrate love set against the special times each month throughout 1992.

Next month... If Maggie knew college men looked this good, she'd've gone back to school years ago. Now forty and about to become a grandma, can she handle these sexy young men? Find out in:

SEPTEMBER

**SAND MAN
by Tracy Hughes**

Read all the Calendar of Romance titles, coming to you one per month, all year, only in American Romance.
